Kaidyn is the son of the queen and a trainee officer in the kingdom of Sareen. He is also a Half-Blood—his father is from Iskandir, a neighboring kingdom which has been at war with Sareen for many years. Bitter and angry at the prejudice he faces, Kaidyn meets Sorin, a healer from one of Sareen's most prominent noble families. As their relationship deepens, the war between Sareen and Iskandir grows worse. Not only will the pair inevitably become involved with the conflict one way or another, but Sorin is also hiding a secret, and time is running out for them both.

Kaidyn's Courage
Copyright © 2019 Diana Waters
ISBN: 978-1-4874-2374-2
Cover art by Erin Dameron-Hill

Published by eXtasy Books Inc or
Devine Destinies, an imprint of eXtasy Books Inc

Look for us online at:
www.eXtasybooks.com or www.devinedestinies.com

Kaidyn's Courage
Wild Magics Book 2

By

Diana Waters

DEDICATION

To Christina, my gratifyingly enthusiastic beta reader, and to Tim, who has now been awarded the illustrious office of Advisor for War — even though man-pr0n is (still) not his thing.

CHAPTER ONE

"And so Brave Kaidyn, with a last burst of strength, plunged his sword deep into the dragon's breast, piercing its heart and killing the great beast where it stood, and the kingdom was safe once more."

His mother closed the book, though the boy continued to see in his mind the final images of the story, his own face painted onto the hero-knight's. This took little effort, for the tale was as familiar to him as the touch of his mother's hand. "And like Brave Kaidyn, it is time now to rest."

"Just one more?" he pleaded.

"Not tonight, dear. You have a big day tomorrow. Now, give your mother a hug." She leaned down, pressing her cheek against his, and he wrapped his arms around her before stiffening and pulling away.

"I'll be eight summers old in the morning! Aren't I too old for hugs?" he asked, anxious.

His mother laughed and shook her head, dislodging several hairpins and setting more strands of dark hair tumbling loose. "Neither of my children," she said, voice fond, "will ever be too old for hugs."

"Oh." He relaxed, then yawned as she released him. "Mother, since tomorrow is my name day, do you think I could write a message to father?"

" . . . Of course, my darling. If you like."

"Because he is the one who named me, you're always telling me so," he said eagerly.

"That's right. He chose the name so you would become brave and strong and good, just like the knight in the story."

1

"And one day he might come home so I can meet him myself!"

"Wouldn't that be lovely?" his mother agreed.

Kaidyn wriggled with excitement at the thought. He had no memory of his father, and there were no paintings of him in the palace. However, his mother often said he had given Kaidyn his looks — his height, dusky skin, and his light brown eyes that were almost amber in color — though she claimed not to know where her son had inherited such extraordinary hair.

"Like red wine." She would laugh, delighted. "My summer berry child."

Kaidyn could see no face but his own in the mirror, but he liked the idea that his father had given him something before he had gone away. His father must have been a great man, Kaidyn was sure, since nobody who liked stories about Kaidyn the Brave could ever be bad.

"Oh! And if he comes back then he'll want to marry you again! I've never seen a wedding before," Kaidyn mused. "You had better not marry anyone else then, mother. Everyone in the Council wants you to marry someone else, but I know you don't really want to."

The hand that had been stroking his head stilled. "Where did you hear that, my sweet?"

"I heard you and Lyrah talking when I was hiding from Luck. Lyrah never wants to play with me anymore," he added, more subdued now.

"Your sister is wise beyond her years," his mother replied after a moment. "Wiser than I. She will make a fine ruler someday." Then she smiled down at him again. "But she does not know everything yet. And we'll just have to keep that our little secret."

Kaidyn smiled back, reassured. "Don't worry, mother. I won't tell anyone, I'm good at keeping secrets!"

"I know you are. Just like that broken vase under your pillow yesterday, hmm?" She only laughed again when he shifted guiltily and began pulling back the bed covers. "I'll tell you what. I won't tell if you won't. Now, it really is time to sleep."

"Yes, mother." He scrambled beneath the coverlet and watched *as she stood in a rustle of silk, one hand covering a yawn, before picking up the candlestick and walking to the door. There she paused a moment, reaching out to touch a vase of wilting flowers perched on a nearby chest of drawers as Kaidyn settled himself. Her sleeve fell back, revealing the tattoo on her wrist, a clear mark of her status as Gifted. The air shimmered as her Gift passed from hand to petals, imparting them with life so that they stood fresh and bright once more.*

"Ready?"

"Yes. Good night, mother." Despite his earlier excitement, his eyes were already starting to feel heavy.

"Good night, Kaidyn."

She blew out the candles and closed the door behind her, and his eyes drifted closed. He slept, and dreamed that he was no mere child but Kaidyn the Brave, swinging his legendary sword and hunting down rampaging dragons, riding valiantly into battle and running, running . . .

Kaidyn was running.

Boots thumping on the uneven cobblestones, he darted around townspeople. He ran past rows of street merchants loudly hawking their wares, a band of children playing games with small colored stones, a pair of squabbling old women.

A hunk of meat was roasting on a spit, its owner trying—and failing—to keep the flies away. A small gang of sharp-eyed boys watched passersby, perhaps on the lookout for a rich pocket to pick, while a group of heavily bearded men threw cards at a rickety table. Nearby, a baby wailed in the arms of a woman who might have been its mother or its sister, attempting in vain to quiet it.

Not a drop of rain had fallen in weeks, and the earth was dry as a bone. Swirling dust and dirt and gods knew what else made Kaidyn want to shield his mouth. All the surrounding sights, smells, and sounds enveloped him, swallowing him up until he was just one of many, vanishing in the swarm of bodies.

Somewhere in front and a little to the right of him, Luck let out an exuberant whoop as though he was running a race instead of running from his superiors. "Lost 'em, Kai!" he shouted above the din. He slowed around the next corner and Kaidyn caught up to walk alongside him, eventually stopping to lean up against the shade of a twisted door frame. Luck thumped down beside him, grinning. "Told you it would work."

Kaidyn felt the corners of his mouth tilt upwards in response despite himself. "You did," he agreed. "Care to tell me how you escaped your own quarters?"

"Maybe I came up with such a good distraction they never even saw me leave."

Kaidyn raised an eyebrow.

"Or maybe I seduced one of the guards," Luck continued, batting his eyelashes in an unconvincing display of flirtatiousness. "Hinted at my many charms."

"Really."

"Oh, all right. Someone did show off their charms, but it wasn't me. I called in a favor from a friend. A very well-endowed friend, if you must know."

"Ah. That makes more sense." Luck's particular brand of roguish appeal had always made him popular with women, though this one might have been anything from a passing acquaintance to a lover. He often visited the brothels and was familiar with many of the workers there, men and women both.

"I'll have you know I happen to be very seductive when I put my mind to it."

"I'm sure."

Luck grinned again, pushing unruly curls from his eyes.

Though Kaidyn didn't say it, he had missed his childhood

friend. Now that they were separated by different training schools, it had been several weeks since their last meeting.

As far as Kaidyn was concerned, Luck had been one of the sole joys to result from moving permanently to the capital as a child. The looming threat of war with Iskandir had finally become serious enough for the family to abandon their less grand yet far more private summer palace in the north. By comparison, the capital had seemed overly large and unfriendly. Even his sister, whom Kaidyn had idolized, appeared to grow cold and remote almost overnight.

The other children living in and around the palace were minor relatives and little lords or ladies in their own right. They took cues from their elders and kept their distance from him. Everyone was aware that although Kaidyn was a prince, he was unable to inherit, even had he been the eldest child. Anyone in good standing knew the Half-Blood would never have any significant role in matters of state or the court. His father's ancestry saw to that.

But Luck had been as different from them as day from night. Tall and lanky, he was a slightly wild boy even then with his head of shorn, tight brown curls and laughing eyes almost exactly the same shade as Kaidyn's own. If not for his distinctly rough manner of speech, they might even have passed as brothers. Certainly Kaidyn resembled Luck far more than he did Lyrah, who was as small as her mother, but had inherited her late father's slenderness and sea-green eyes. Kaidyn had been in awe of his new friend, so different from any other he had known and with an unquestionable talent for getting into trouble—and usually for skipping neatly out of it again.

They had been utterly inseparable in their youth. As children they had been thick as thieves and cared nothing for their difference in status. When they were together, Kaidyn, the son of the queen, was equal to Luck, the son of an undercook who worked somewhere in the palace's vast kitchens.

As the years passed, however, they experienced a growing awareness of who and what they were in the eyes of the
court. They made a pact not to care about status and shared
a friendly rivalry, fighting over which of them could run
quicker, ride faster or fight harder.

As young men on the verge of adulthood, they had for a
brief time become lovers in the way many others did who
trained or fought away from home. Now, they were closer to
brothers again, protective and goading in equal measures,
and determined to fight the world together.

Luck was still catching his breath as Kaidyn cast a glance
from their makeshift hiding place. He could neither see nor
hear any sign of pursuit, though no doubt at least one or two
of his instructors were among the crowd somewhere, attempting to track him down like some runaway child. Well,
they would be searching a long time. Kaidyn had no intention of returning until much later, long after darkness had
fallen and he would not be bothered by anyone.

With some luck, he might even be able to sleep a few
hours, uninterrupted by others and his ugly thoughts. Even
in the light of day they had a habit of stealing into his head,
making his gut turn sour, his hands curl into fists —

"C'mon, I need a drink." Luck pushed himself back from
the door frame. "On you this time. I'm your dashing savior,
after all, helping you break out of there like the delicate
young flower you are."

Kaidyn grunted but nodded, even as an unwelcome sense
of responsibility nagged at him. He was, despite everything,
a son of the royal family as well as a soldier, and his actions
reflected on them. He shouldn't be worrying his mother,
shaming his sister, giving the Council yet another reason to
despise him by shirking his duties.

"You're doing it again." Luck jostled him playfully, scattering his thoughts.

"Doing what?"

"Overthinking it."

Kaidyn made a conscious effort to relax his shoulders and allowed Luck to sweep them back out into the milling throng. They walked at a slower pace, the crowd swarming around Kaidyn as he trailed behind Luck, who led the way to one of their frequent drinking spots. It was not the first time they had passed an evening in such a way—and it would almost certainly not be the last.

But Kaidyn could not fault Luck for trying to distract him and knew that however isolated he might feel, he was not alone in his sense of entrapment. It was like a noose, one that gradually tightened day by day as empty, faceless spectators hissed and jeered. They spat on him, just as they spat on Luck for being somehow lesser than they were in the world. Nobody ever bothered to say less *what* exactly, but Kaidyn already knew without having to be told.

Less noble. Less worthy. Less honorable. A half-breed, with the blood of an enemy nation flowing through his veins. It would have been one thing simply to be unGifted, as many nobles were no matter how high their rank. It was quite another to be a physical reminder to all who looked upon him of his race.

But for all that, he was no noble's pet to whimper and cower, or worse, beg in an effort to please or placate his so-called betters. He would turn on his *masters* and sink his teeth into their flesh before such a day ever came.

Suddenly aware his fingernails had been digging into his palm again, Kaidyn let out a breath in an explosive sigh. At least the tavern would be loud enough that he wouldn't be able to hear himself think. What was one more drink to try and make him forget for a time?

And so he pushed the uninvited thoughts away and followed Luck further into the crowd.

Kaidyn's head snapped back with the force of the punch. He inhaled sharply, but there was no cracking sound — only a brief burst of pain rushing to life, almost welcome in its sharpness. Unable to dodge in time, he at least had the brief satisfaction of hearing the splintering bone of his opponent's fingers.

Right on cue, Luck gave a feral laugh and wiped his nose where blood trickled bright beneath it. He lunged toward their attackers, feinting left and then striking out with his right. There was definitely a crack then, not from Luck's hand, but from their attacker's head as it crashed backward into the nearest table. Kaidyn was not worried. Even drunk, Luck was experienced enough to know how to hold his punches. If they were arrested tonight, it would not be for murder.

"Whad'ya say, Kai?" Luck's voice rose amidst the chaos of roars and clattering tankards, the words slurring together. Two more men had replaced the first. "I take this one, you the other?"

"You'll both take it outside before I call the Watch!" The owner was short and squat, and plainly no stranger to tavern brawls. He shook a meaty fist in Kaidyn's direction. "I know you two! Now out, before you break any more noses. Or my furniture! On the street where you belong, *all* of you!"

"They started it!" someone called out. Kaidyn couldn't tell whose side they were on, but that scarcely mattered now. The anger had taken hold, and he wanted to roar and tear and claw his way to oblivion, black eye be damned.

He couldn't even recall what exactly had sparked it. Some stray remark or other, a barbed comment that might or might not have been directed at them in the first place. Either way, Luck had taken immediate offense and Kaidyn had jumped in to back him up. Then there had been nothing beyond the tight, sweaty press of too many bodies packed into too small a space, the stench of cheap beer, wine, and stronger spirits invading his nostrils.

Someone grabbed at his arm, and Kaidyn shook the hand off impatiently. Luck was swearing, someone had picked up a tankard and looked about to swing it on top of another man's head, and the owner yelled something else as the heap turned into a mob. It moved and swayed, sweeping him outside as numerous voices shouted at once, the words lost to the overall din.

"Luck!" Kaidyn had lost sight of him somewhere in the roiling mass.

"Here!" came the answering call, but it was impossible to tell from where, and then Kaidyn found himself desperately fighting as several men came at him at once. He landed several decent blows before the crush of bodies overwhelmed him, pressing him against hard stone. He tried to swing out again and some idiot crashed into him, laughing crazily and sending him slamming back into the wall. Then his arms were being pinned behind him, and Kaidyn doubled over as he was struck hard in the stomach. He retched, choking as he was released.

"I'll kick your teeth out, filthy Half-Blood!"

"Hands off him you bastards! I said let *go*—" Luck's voice cut off as more scuffling sounds came from around them. The majority of the crowd had parted and was going back inside, but the scrap had become a real fight. Bystanders and casual brawlers scrambled away, back to their drinks or safely into the night, until only the hard-bitten, pinch-faced men accustomed to real violence were left.

"He's not got any money on him lads, might as well let him rot—"

Kaidyn snarled something—he didn't know what—and

straightened up, his leg lashing blindly out. His instincts were sound though, and his knee connected with something solid. A groin, judging by the moan he heard next.

"You little shit—"

"Oi! The Watch, run!"

Kaidyn's ears had caught it, too—the clinking of steel as a patrol wandered nearby, perhaps attracted by the sounds of their struggle. No others could walk the city streets openly armed, even by day. Not that Kaidyn wanted to stick around any longer than his attackers. He had no wish to be locked up for the night either.

The man directly in front of him seized him by the collar of his shirt. "Something to remember me by," he muttered, and Kaidyn knew his mouth was open but couldn't hear his own gasp as he was dealt a final blow. The hit wasn't in his stomach again, as he'd been expecting, but at the side of his head. It felt like an object struck him, not merely a fist, but something blunt and hard. He felt the blood begin to drip from the base of his skull and trickle down his neck. The world wavered around him as the last of the men ran off. *Cowards, all.*

Kaidyn took an uneven step, then several more. He tilted toward the ground but did not fall. *Luck. Where is Luck? I have to find him, before . . .*

He was still so angry, but his thoughts were leaking out of him along with the blood, the dizziness beginning to consume them. *If I don't hurry . . .*

The stars were wheeling somewhere above him. *When did I fall to the ground?* He tried to search for a familiar landmark, but his sight was failing him. Kaidyn had either drank too much or been hit too hard.

"Oh!" Kaidyn heard a gasp, but it had not come from him. It wasn't Luck, either. He tried to get up, to defend himself once more, but his hands met only empty air.

"I'm not going to hurt you, I promise—"

Kaidyn growled, his tone low and furious.

"All right, all right," the voice soothed him. "I'll just wait until you're ready to walk again, shall I?" The unknown person sounded sympathetic. Gentle, even, and impossibly, unbearably kind. But that must have been in his head, because surely nobody who saw Kaidyn in his current state could be anything but disappointed, disgusted, or a combination of the two.

"It's going to be all right," the voice continued, and to Kaidyn's astonishment he felt a cool hand touching his brow, brushing wisps of hair from his forehead. He could not remember the last time he had been touched with such tenderness. "I have you. You're safe now. I won't leave you alone here."

Kaidyn shook his head, forcing his sight to clear. A pair of eyes stared anxiously back down at him and drew him in, as though calling him on from somewhere. But from where? Where . . .

Kai!

He had definitely imagined that part, because this stranger, whoever he was, could not have known his name, much less the one reserved for his closest friends.

Kai!

But he could not think any longer, he was falling, falling . . . and running again, running away from the pain and the bile rising in his throat, escaping everything but the darkness that finally overtook him to swallow him whole.

CHAPTER TWO

Water.

That was Kaidyn's first thought after dragging himself back from the void. It was like being pulled out of a deep river after being submerged for some time—he felt weak and shaky, but clean, too, newer somehow. Perhaps it was because he could hear actual water from somewhere nearby. Not the rush of a river, but the slow, mesmerizing *plop, plop* of water being wrung into a basin. It was as if whoever was doing it was taking great care to squeeze the cloth just so.

Kaidyn held his breath for a moment as the dripping slowed further and finally ceased altogether. Sure enough, a moment later he felt a damp cloth being pressed to his forehead before it moved down to his eyes, ears, nose, mouth. Kaidyn could think of only one person who would ever touch him in such a manner, but judging from the unmistakably masculine humming that accompanied the action, this was definitely not his mother. Nor could it be Luck—the voice was not pitched deep enough. Besides, his friend would never have handled Kaidyn so gently, as though he might break. Luck's friendship was of a rougher, more familiar sort than that.

Whoever this was did not hesitate to touch him, and it felt strangely intimate—far closer than that of only a relative or friend. *Could it be somebody else I know, or once knew, long ago?* The thought teased at him as Kaidyn tried to place this sense of familiarity, like a voice calling him from somewhere under the river. Quiet but insistent, it whispered his name as though it were one to be loved and treasured. *Kai.*

Impossible. There is no such person.

At the thought, Kaidyn's eyes snapped open and the humming broke off.

"You're awake!" the voice said instead, surprise and concern mingling together. "I thought you would sleep a while still. It is not yet dawn."

Kaidyn's sight was blurry, still adjusting to the candlelight that greeted him, but he could not blink, could not even draw breath for a moment as he stared, transfixed, at the boy.

No, not the boy, Kaidyn corrected himself. The man. He was young, yes, but not that young. The open expression had fooled him for a moment, but the face framed by a spill of black hair was too lean to be a child's, and the marks of exhaustion under his eyes lent further gravity to his features.

"Who . . ." Kaidyn's voice came out husky and strained, and he hid a wince as he swallowed. His head began to pound in earnest and his body to ache as soon as he spoke, dragging him back to the present.

"Here. Drink." The man's distress was plain to see and the hard, obstinate part of Kaidyn wanted to resist, to pull back immediately from such worry for his own well-being. He was not accustomed to it, though this person obviously meant him no harm. His hand shook as he lifted the proffered cup to his lips.

"I'm Sorin," his rescuer spoke again.

Sorin. Not so much unusual as old-fashioned. Traditional. It originated from Sareen, the name of the kingdom itself, but Kaidyn could put no tangible memory to it. This man had to be a lord of some kind, although Kaidyn was already certain he was not from the capital. Sorin's speech was lightly accented — a northerner, perhaps — and in any case, Kaidyn knew every castle inhabitant and their hangers-on at

13

least by face, if not by name or title. Though his personal acquaintances were few and far between, Kaidyn would have bet his own name that they had never previously met.

"My lord, I—"

"Just Sorin, please," the younger man smiled.

"Sorin . . ." Kaidyn prompted.

"Perhaps you might tell me *your* name first." Amusement laced Sorin's tone.

Belatedly, Kaidyn realized he had not yet introduced himself. But then . . ."You don't know it?"

"No. Should I?"

"I thought I heard you call me by it before, when . . . when you found me. But . . ." He stopped, uncertain now that he tried to recall the exact moment.

"You were nearly unconscious at the time. I didn't think you could hear me say anything. In any case, I do not know your name." Sorin looked at him, the hint of a smile still playing about his mouth. "Unless of course you would rather not tell me."

He found himself returning that smile despite himself. "Kaidyn. My name is Kaidyn."

"Kaidyn," Sorin repeated. "Like the knight from the stories?"

"So I was told as a boy. But friends call me Kai," he volunteered, astonishing himself. What had possessed him to say *that*? He allowed scarcely anyone to call him this, and only Luck now referred to him as Kai with any regularity. Had anybody else tried, Kaidyn would probably have struck them. As it was, he felt the words tumble from his mouth with surprising ease.

"Kai it is, then," Sorin said, and Kaidyn felt something he could not name well up inside of him.

Then the pain returned from wherever it had receded with full force, and he knew no more for a time.

He must have slept again, for when he once more became fully aware of his surroundings, the sun was shining bright through the window. Dawn had long since passed, and by Kaidyn's best guess it was approaching mid-morning.

He turned his head to see Sorin kneeling on the floor with his legs folded neatly beneath him, upper body resting on the bed and head pillowed atop his arms. He was breathing deeply and evenly, his eyes closed. Kaidyn watched them flutter beneath their lids as though he was caught in a dream. He had an irrational urge to reach out and touch Sorin, although wariness would have held him back even if habit had not. It went beyond strange, though the feeling was not wholly unpleasant.

In fact, now that Kaidyn thought about it, he felt remarkably well. His head was clear—clearer than it had been in weeks. He reached up to touch it, but there was no bandage. Perhaps the wound had not been as bad as he imagined. There had seemed to be a lot of blood, but he could hardly have been thinking straight at the time. He must have been mistaken.

Still, his body seemed lighter, somehow freer than he remembered. A certain languidness about his limbs suggested that he had been lying still for some time, but the pain, the sharp pounding in his skull, had vanished entirely.

He must have made some small sound.

Sorin stirred then, groaning a little as he awoke. "Umm ... Kai? I apologize, I must have fallen asleep after you ... oh, you look much better!" He smiled even as a yawn overtook him.

"I *feel* better," Kaidyn replied honestly, and witnessed the smile grow in response. Then it disappeared as Sorin clutched his head, gasping a little in what was clearly pain. Kaidyn's hand reached for Sorin's shoulder almost before he became conscious of putting it there. "What's wrong?"

"Nothing . . . a headache, that's all. They're common enough, it will pass."

"You're pale. Here, drink."

Kaidyn had reached for the water beside the bed, instinctively offering it to Sorin, and they both stared at it wordlessly for a moment before his host broke the silence with a laugh. "It seems our roles have been reversed." He took the glass with fingers that trembled slightly, making the water ripple. The circles under his eyes seemed more pronounced than they had earlier.

Kaidyn wondered if Sorin was ill, then frowned at the thought. It was none of his business, and not in his nature to be so curious of strangers. "How did I get here? And how long have I been asleep?" he asked, in part to mask his unease.

"I . . . ah, commandeered some help, more or less." Sorin looked abashed. "The City Watch," he explained at Kaidyn's puzzled expression,

Kaidyn's heart sank. If the Watch had recognized him, then word about what had passed would almost certainly get back to his mother as well as the Council. He wondered what Sorin had told them.

"You've been asleep several hours," Sorin was continuing. "I went out for a few moments to fetch some things, and you hadn't moved at all by the time I returned. Which reminds me — somebody was looking for you."

"Oh? Who?" Kaidyn tried to appear nonchalant, but if the wry humor in Sorin's face was anything to go by, he clearly saw through the façade.

"Not the Watch," he said. "A lone man. About your age and height, I think. He had short brown hair, the curliest I've ever seen, and something of a . . . a rakish look to him."

Kaidyn could not help but grin at the description. Yes,

that was Luck exactly. "A friend," he told Sorin. "Does he know where I am?"

"No. We did not speak. I only overheard him asking another about you as I was passing by, not too far from where I found you last night. He did not mention you by name, but I was certain he could not be talking of anyone else."

"He's all right then," Kaidyn said with some relief. "We got separated in the fight and I couldn't get to him."

Sorin raised his brows. "I won't pretend to be surprised, though I can't say I approve of fighting. But . . . well, I suppose you gave as good as you got?"

"I didn't think I had," Kaidyn admitted. "Call it a brawl rather than a fight, and we the only two against a crowd. But I felt a lot worse last night than I do now. I suppose I can't have been injured as badly as all that."

"Then I'm glad." Sorin started to get up, but there was a pinched look around his mouth as though he was holding in another gasp. He mastered himself quickly enough, but Kaidyn noted that Sorin kept a hand on the bed to steady himself as he stood.

Biting his tongue against prying questions, Kaidyn instead chose to voice the next one that occurred to him. "Where are my clothes?"

Inexplicably, Sorin blushed. "I took them to be washed. They looked like they needed it."

"Oh." Kaidyn was unfazed. Nudity did not bother him. Self-consciousness had no place in a soldier's life, and men in his position tended to lose it fairly quickly. When you were surrounded by other men for weeks or months at a time, there was simply no other choice. Still, he found Sorin's obvious embarrassment rather charming. It had been a long time since Kaidyn had observed such modesty. "Thank you," he added somewhat belatedly.

"It was my pleasure. Ah . . . do you want them back now?

17

They were returned a short while ago, and if your friend is out looking for you . . ."

The old heaviness came back at the thought of returning to the training school. Back to tedious and relentless drill work, despite the fact that Kaidyn was already far more skilled than any of his fellow trainees.

Back to the silent scorn of his peers, who never hesitated to hiss their contempt for him under their breath. Kaidyn was far from the only man of mixed blood in the city, but he was certainly the only one at the academy. To sons, brothers, nephews and cousins of nobility, his odd position among them as a member of the court with no land, no title, and no chance of inheritance made him a clear target for their derision. The anger stirred up in his chest at the memories, begging once more to be let out where it could growl and snap and snarl its fury.

"Kai?" Sorin was watching him closely. "If you'd like to stay a while longer, you could . . . that is, I'm not — "

"My lord. I thank you for the kind offer, but I must be on my way," Kaidyn interrupted, and watched Sorin draw back as sharply as though he had slapped him. His expression showed hurt at the sudden cool formality before it was wiped away, leaving his features schooled to neutrality.

"Very well. I will bring you your clothes and give you some privacy."

Sorin withdrew and Kaidyn immediately wanted to snatch back his words. *What am I doing, being intentionally callous like this — and to the man who took me from the streets and offered me shelter for the night, no less?* Yet he was unwilling to call Sorin back.

Such a man was not someone Kaidyn should be on such casual terms with, or on any terms at all, for that matter. Sorin was patently someone of high status. His bearing, the way he spoke, the pale skin and color of his hair and eyes all but screamed nobility to Kaidyn, who had grown up as both one of and yet outside the aristocracy, and who could spot any one of them a mile away.

It wasn't just about money or how well one was dressed. It was the way your nobility *belonged* to you, as instinctive and natural as drawing breath. Either you had it or you did not, and Sorin unquestionably did. Son of the queen Kaidyn might be, but as a Half-Blood who possessed no skills to speak of beyond those with a sword, he was almost laughably beneath someone of Sorin's social position. If Sorin had known who Kaidyn was, he would not even have deigned to speak with him, let alone tend to him as he had. Kaidyn was not and would never be worth such care.

He tried to brush the thought away as he tugged on his trousers and fastened his shirt. Sorin had brought his clothes before quickly retreating once more, and Kaidyn noted that they looked and smelled as fresh as if they were new. Just one more thing to thank Sorin for — *Lord* Sorin, that was. He ran a hand through hair cropped defiantly short, much too short to be properly bound in the manner of a nobleman. But there was little to be done about it beyond attempting to smooth it down and hoping he passed as at least somewhat presentable.

When Kaidyn finished dressing, he left the bedchamber and made his way through the otherwise strangely empty house. It was not overly large, even rather small in comparison to what he had been expecting, but surely Sorin didn't live alone. He must have servants at least. Yet there were no footsteps to be heard other than Kaidyn's own — barely any sign that the place was inhabited at all, much less by someone of Sorin's status.

The man in question was waiting for him in what must have been the parlor, though it too was small and sparsely furnished. Sorin appeared neither angry nor upset as he accompanied Kaidyn to the door, instead offering him a tremulous smile. "I suppose . . . we may not see each other again. This is not a small town."

"No, my lord," Kaidyn agreed. "I am at the officer's academy most of the time for training in any case."

Sorin's eyes lit up unexpectedly at the words. "Then we will most certainly meet again! I'm to begin work there in a few days."

"Work?" Kaidyn was bewildered. In his experience, the vast majority of those of noble birth did no such thing.

"Yes," Sorin replied happily, oblivious to Kaidyn's bewilderment. "And I'm sure the academy can't be all that large, though I haven't had occasion to visit just yet. I look forward to it."

He opened the door, and Kaidyn could immediately see that they were not very far from the edge of the town—he could already hear the faint cries of market vendors, see the clouds of dust in the distance kicked up by the morning crowds. Somewhere among them, Luck was probably still searching.

"I must go. I'm sorry, I—"

"It's all right." Sorin's hand closed around his own, and his head tilted back slightly so that he was staring directly into Kaidyn's eyes.

Kaidyn stared back, pulled in by Sorin's gaze, unable to turn away.

"Kaidyn Riverveil," Sorin murmured. His stare had become empty. Startlingly empty. "So proud. Yet so angry. Kaidyn, will you let it all go someday?"

"I—what?" The shock of it made the back of Kaidyn's neck prickle.

Then Sorin was shaking his head as if clearing it, the awful blankness vanishing as swiftly as it had arrived as his expression grew rueful. "Now I'm the one who's sorry.

Sometimes my mind plays tricks on me, and I speak without really knowing what I say." He seemed to become aware that they were still holding hands, releasing his grip as Kaidyn pulled away in confusion. "I'll see you soon. Be well, Kai."

He left Kaidyn gaping at a closed door, listening as Sorin's footsteps faded away from inside.

What did he mean, we will see each other again? Sorin was no soldier, of that Kaidyn was sure. No instructor either, surely, and certainly not a cook or any other manner of servant. *A tactician, perhaps? Or some kind of envoy?* But that did not seem quite right, either. Kaidyn began to walk, barely noticing anything beyond a step in front of him as the questions swirled in his mind.

It was not until several minutes later, just before catching sight of a familiar head of wild curls and calling out to his friend, that Kaidyn finally realized he had not thought to ask again for Sorin's full name.

And it was not until that night, tossing and turning back in his bed at the academy, that Kaidyn wondered just how Sorin had come to know his.

CHAPTER THREE

"So? You going to tell me or not?"

"Tell you what?" Kaidyn was perfectly aware of what, and he knew Luck did as well.

His friend huffed impatiently. "This mystery man of yours, what else? You've still said near to nothing about him."

Kaidyn shrugged. He had indeed said little about the encounter after taking his leave of Sorin a few days earlier. Luck only knew that he had been pulled from the street at some point after the fight, and that he did not know his rescuer. His best friend—who was all too familiar with the set of Kaidyn's shoulders—hadn't asked any more questions that day. They had walked in silence until the tall walls and imposing gate of the officer's academy cast shadows over the pair. Here they parted ways, Luck returning to his own training barracks where many young men of low birth, mixed blood, or both inevitably found themselves for the promise of food, shelter, and a small amount of coin. For once, Kaidyn had been glad for their enforced separation. After assuring himself that Luck had gotten away from the fight with nothing worse than a few bruises and one or two dislocated fingers, the only thing Kaidyn had wished for was solitude.

The encounter with Sorin held a dreamlike quality to it, making Kaidyn half-wonder if he had imagined the entire thing. Even to himself, the events surrounding the meeting sounded like something out of a tale. He couldn't shake the feeling that the more he spoke of it, the less he would re-member. Now that several days had passed, Kaidyn knew he could no longer avoid the conversation. No matter how unwilling he was to speak of it, Luck deserved answers.

"Not much to tell," he replied finally. "He was . . . kind, that's all."

Luck snorted. "*Kind* doesn't begin to cover it. How often does some stranger—someone of noble blood, I might add—drag in a drunk and unconscious soldier from the street? He sounds more crazy than anything else, or like he had some ulterior motive."

"I don't think he knew I was a soldier at the time," Kaidyn said. He paused, then went on, "I doubt he knew anything about me. He certainly wasn't from around here. He mustn't have realized . . ."

Kaidyn didn't need to finish the sentence for Luck to understand. *Half-Blood.* Luck was right—the stigma against men such as them meant that it wasn't just unlikely, but virtually unbelievable, for someone of nobility to stoop to saving one of their kind.

Luck gave a noncommittal grunt. "You said he called himself Sorin. Common enough name, so that's no good. Family name?"

Kaidyn was silent. Luck studied him for a moment, then laughed disbelievingly. "You're joking. You don't know?"

"He didn't give it to me."

"And you didn't ask?" Luck was incredulous. "What, did getting your head knocked in deprive you of your common sense?"

"Leave it," Kaidyn warned.

If he was honest, it wasn't just the surrealism of the encounter that held him back from speaking more freely. He was feeling oddly defensive about the whole experience and had no desire to share any more than was necessary. His time with Sorin seemed . . . private somehow, even sacred. Their time together was something he didn't want to reveal to the rest of the world—not even to Luck, who for years had been his closest friend and the single person in whom Kaidyn could confide.

Only Luck could understand the true extent of his frustration, anger and shame, for he felt it all, too. But the details of his encounter with Sorin, even though nothing had happened that should have caused Kaidyn to feel embarrassed or secretive, seemed too intimate to share.

"At least tell me more about the man," Luck prodded. "What business does he have here if he doesn't belong with any of those fools up at the palace? What did he look like?"

Kaidyn frowned, this time in thought. "I don't know what he's doing here. He said something about work at the officer's academy, but I have no idea what he was talking about. I didn't recognize the name either, but it could be he has family here. As for his appearance . . ." He hesitated.

"What? Was he really that strange?"

"He . . . no. Not strange exactly, just . . . I don't know. Striking, I suppose." He tried to focus on the concrete details. "Very pale. Dark hair, quite long. Dark blue eyes."

"Mm. Doesn't exactly help much. That could be almost anyone."

"I know. And he didn't mention any relatives, either."

Luck looked at him, a sly expression coming over his face. "Was he handsome?"

Kaidyn had no answer to that. *Handsome*, just like *kind*, didn't even come close, but not because of Sorin's looks. It was just that it was the wrong word entirely to describe him—although he couldn't think of the right word to use in its stead. It went beyond Sorin's hair and eye color, although that in itself was undeniably fine.

Neither did it have anything to do with his stature, which

Kaidyn had thought pleasant enough but otherwise unexceptional. From what he remembered, Sorin had not been
particularly tall, and had what Kaidyn deemed a slight but
unremarkable build. No, there had been something else
about Sorin that had little, if anything, to do with physical
appearance. Sorin had a certain air, a presence, which had
drawn Kaidyn in despite his sound instincts. It had been
something almost unearthly, as though Sorin trod a fine line
between this world and another. Even to Kaidyn, such a description seemed ridiculously fanciful, and he would have
once laughed at such a thing. *And yet . . .*

"Fine, keep it to yourself then," Luck grumbled. "I see I'll
be getting no more out of you — for now, at least. I'll give this
to your mysterious beauty though, he did a decent enough
job of patching you up. Hardly a scratch on you."

That was yet another point that had been nagging at him.
Luck was right. After returning to the training school and
thoroughly inspecting his body for damage, Kaidyn had
been surprised to discover how little evidence remained of
the previous night. He had been hit squarely in the stomach,
of that much he was certain. The blow had been hard
enough to make him double over in pain. The knock to his
head had also been severe enough to break the skin and
eventually render him senseless. But looking over his image
in the mirror with a critical eye, all Kaidyn had found were
several already fading bruises and a thin, slightly bloody
gash that was too minor even for stitches.

Reason told him that his whole body should have ached,
and indeed, Kaidyn distinctly remembered that it had the
first time he woke up. Since then, however, it was almost as
though the fight had never happened.

Of course, it was possible to chalk up his wounds — or
lack thereof — to seeming far more severe than they really
had been due to the alcohol, his practically guaranteed con-

cussion, or both. But this didn't seem quite right to Kaidyn either, even though he was unable to explain precisely why this was so. Not for the first time, he wondered if he had simply dreamed most of it up while he was still out cold. The hallucinatory effects of blood loss combined with too much to drink could have seen to that. After all, Sorin had said—or at least, Kaidyn *thought* he had—that they would see each other again at the academy. Yet he had not caught a single glimpse of Sorin since, nor heard mention of his name.

Luck eventually gave up. "Be sure to tell me if your dark too-handsome-for-words paramour makes a comeback," he said, leaving Kaidyn to mull over Luck's sardonic parting words.

Back at the academy, Kaidyn chafed under his continued punishment for leaving the school without permission, for breaking curfew, and for engaging in *drunken and violent behavior unbecoming of a trainee officer* by running laps around the grounds under an unrelenting sun. But whether it was doing this, cleaning the school's training equipment to the meticulous standards of the instructors, or any of the other dozen tedious tasks they could come up with as penalty for his actions, Kaidyn didn't care so long as he was left to do it alone. Nonetheless, his sentence struck him as utterly pointless. It was an exercise that served only to make him more withdrawn and did not instill any sense of regret or remorse. The more they pushed, the more he pulled away. His instructors, Kaidyn seethed, were fools if they could not see this.

He was called back indoors nearly an hour later, drenched in sweat and made to line up with the other trainees, who either pointedly ignored him or uttered choice remarks under their breath. Kaidyn refused to even meet their eyes and stood staring straight ahead, but he could not close his ears. He wondered whether some day he might simply crack with the effort of keeping all of his fury pent up inside, just as the string of a bow drawn taut enough would eventually, inexorably, snap.

Someone bellowed for silence. Kaidyn looked up through the ranks from his position near the back to where the head instructor was climbing onto the wooden platform.

"I have a brief announcement to make," he began. His voice echoed clearly through the hall. "Today we welcome a new face among us. He is here as apprentice healer and physicker, where he is to learn under Mistress Nora and help with her work in the infirmary. I expect everyone to heed and obey any of his instructions in the same manner you do Mistress Nora's. If you please?" he turned, nodding to a figure behind him.

His hair was loose before, Kaidyn thought numbly as the unmistakable figure stepped up to join the instructor on the stage. Unbound, it had fallen like a dark pool about his shoulders, but Sorin was no less recognizable now that it was tugged back into a simple braid, just as Nora's always was—like the few healers at the palace had always worn theirs. Curse it, if it had been braided when they had first met then Kaidyn would have guessed—he would have immediately made the connection and known the truth.

The head instructor was continuing to speak. "May I introduce to you all to Lord—" Sorin turned and interrupted him, murmuring something in a low voice to the instructor. His expression and body language were respectful but firm.

"Sorin," the instructor finished somewhat awkwardly, his brows drawing together. He was clearly incapable of understanding why a nobleman would wish to disregard his rightful title. "Needless to say, he will be treated with the utmost respect." He stepped to the side, gesturing for Sorin to say a few words in response.

Kaidyn watched intently as Sorin seemed to scan the crowd before inclining his head courteously. "I thank you for your kind welcome," he said. His voice was not overly loud, but Kaidyn heard every syllable as clearly as the strike of a bell, and his heart hammered suddenly and almost painfully in response. "And I look forward to getting to know you all in time. Please, do not hesitate to speak with me about anything you may need. I will be glad to be of help." His simple speech ended, Sorin stepped back, though he continued to scour the crowd before him.

The moment his gaze met Kaidyn's stare, Sorin's face lit up as though he had just been given the world, and all Kaidyn could do was gape back at his rescuer as the world lurched around him.

Kaidyn paced the hallways restlessly that evening, unable to remain still. Not only was Sorin a noble, he was Gifted as well, and a *healer* of all things. A powerful one too, if he had truly healed the worst of the injures from the tavern in the space of an hour or two.

" . . . Had not realized there were quite so many trainees." Sorin's voice filtered out from the main room of the infirmary, and Kaidyn jerked to a stop like a puppet on strings. On his last passing—which coincidentally was the fourth time he had found an excuse to walk by that very door the same evening—the room had been empty. He had not really been expecting anything else now.

"Nearly two hundred of them currently enrolled in this school," Nora replied. "I'm glad you answered my letter and arrived as quickly you did, cousin. I could use the extra pair of hands."

"But there can't be that many injuries?"

"Fewer than you might think. Their time here is spent on furthering their training, not beginning it. But accidents happen. And with so many bodies living in close quarters, over a long period of time . . . sickness can spread all too easily."

"I need to study how to better cope with that especially," said Sorin, earnestly. "Sickness is so much more challenging for me than physical injury. Though of course," he added hurriedly, "I know I still have much to learn in all areas."

"You have a deft touch," Nora said matter-of-factly. "And while you lack experience, you're also one of the strongest healers I know. Most at the palace are of moderate ability at best, albeit formally trained, and it pleases its inhabitants to have them on hand. Continue your own training, and there will come a day you'll easily surpass both them and me."

"Oh! I don't think . . . I mean, I'm not quite . . ." Their conversation faded into the background as cupboards were opened and shut, glass jars clinking softly and wooden surfaces squeaking as they were scrubbed down for the night.

" . . . Under control? . . . headaches . . ."

Kaidyn took an involuntarily step closer before halting again, tempted to turn away now before he heard any more. It was none of his business, and regardless, eavesdropping was a deplorable habit. Leave that to snooping nobles currying favor or gleaning ill-gotten secrets. And yet, Kaidyn also knew he would be lying if he told himself he didn't wish to know more about Sorin.

No matter how much he tried to fight the mesmerizing pull the healer had on him, Kaidyn was intrigued. He couldn't begin to describe or rationalize the healer's pull on him and knew that it went beyond mere fascination. Kaidyn had experienced infatuation, sexual attraction, even love before. Still, nothing came close to defining whatever had come over him now. It was ridiculous, especially considering that the amount of time he had personally spent in Sorin's presence came to only a few short hours. Less, if you counted the fact that Kaidyn had been unconscious for most of it.

Ridiculous, wonderful, and utterly terrifying.

" . . . Until now. But . . . again recently. I'm almost certain . . . caught me unawares before, though mercifully not often."

Kaidyn's muscles were beginning to ache from the effort of standing so still. A part of him wanted to run and keep running until he had left this place, Sorin, and everything else far behind him. He didn't want to be vulnerable like this, to lay himself so bare. But another part of him refused to budge from this spot, lurking like a common thief, stealing all he could of Sorin's mysteries. Kaidyn barely knew this nobleman, and already he wanted to learn all there was to know of him, inside and out.

He swallowed, throat dry, as Nora spoke again. "Perhaps that too is something we may be able to train," he heard her suggest, her voice coming clearer as they moved closer to the door.

"No. I don't think so." All trace of levity had vanished from Sorin's voice. "I was taught not to squander what I have been given," he went on. "But I never asked for this. Never wanted it. Not for a moment."

"Sorin . . ."

Nora sounded like she wanted to say more but Sorin broke in. "If it's all right with you, cousin, might I take my leave? Unless you need me for anything else, of course."

Kaidyn slowly began backing away, further into the shadows. He heard Nora sigh. "No. No, I don't think so. Get some rest. You look like you need it . . . And Sorin?"

Kaidyn paused, on the verge of retreating fully as Sorin's booted footsteps halted by the entranceway. "Yes?"

"We all have to stop running away sometime. As of now, that time is up to you. But it may be best to do so sooner rather than later. Before you no longer have the freedom to choose."

Kaidyn slipped away before he could overhear any more or be caught listening in to a conversation clearly not meant for anyone else's ears—but he could not quite keep himself from lingering to watch Sorin leave the academy for the day, dark-cloaked and silhouetted against the setting sun.

CHAPTER FOUR

Kaidyn knocked on the door to the infirmary, pretending like he didn't have to forcibly steady his breathing. It didn't matter what Sorin's expression would be when it opened, if he smiled when he saw Kaidyn, or which words he used in greeting. This was of course assuming the man was even there—doubtless he also had responsibilities elsewhere, or he was too busy to speak with him at all.

"Kai!" Sorin emerged from one of the smaller storerooms leading further back into the infirmary. He didn't just look pleased to see Kaidyn. He looked delighted, his smile radiant. Kaidyn didn't know whether he wanted to move closer or run away while he still had the chance—*if* he still had the chance. "I'm so glad you're here!"

"You're . . . you are?" Kaidyn couldn't remember the last time he had felt caught so off balance.

"Of course! When I didn't see you again after being formally introduced to the academy yesterday, I thought that perhaps—well, I'm just glad to see you."

"Can I ask you something?"

"Of course." Despite the abrupt shift in conversation, he remained polite. "Why don't you come in and sit down?"

In contrast, Kaidyn knew he was being rude. *What right do I of all people have to question Sorin?* By anyone's standards, he was behaving discourteously, barging in like this and pressing the healer with questions he was probably uncomfortable answering. Still, after another near-sleepless night, Kaidyn knew nothing could be done but to ask Sorin directly.

"I wanted to thank you again for the other day," he said, finding he couldn't bring himself to sit. He stood in front of Sorin instead, hands balled into fists to keep them from twitching.

"It was my pleasure. I wanted to help."

"You healed me." He tried to keep his voice neutral.

"Yes. I hope you don't mind. But you were already losing consciousness when I found you. I could not have simply left—"

"Mind? Why would I mind?"

For the first time Sorin looked a little uncomfortable. "It's just that . . . well, you didn't even know me, and it's customary to ask permission first if at all possible. And I know that I sometimes—that is, I understand if people might not like it when I act without—"

"But why me?" Kaidyn interrupted again, annoyed as much by himself as by Sorin's fumbling, and not knowing why.

Sorin looked at him, nonplussed. "I already told you. You were lying right there in the street and—"

"Not that. Why *me?*"

"I'm afraid I don't know what you mean," said Sorin helplessly.

"You don't know who I am."

"Nothing other than your name and that you're a trainee here, no," he agreed.

"So even though you somehow know my family name, you're saying you have no idea who *I* am." Kaidyn could not keep the accusatory note from his voice.

"But I don't know your family name," Sorin said, his brow furrowing slightly.

"You called me by it before I left that day. After you healed me. You called me Kaidyn Riverveil."

"I don't remember that."

"You don't remember." Kaidyn could hear himself growing louder, more forceful.

"No."

"You don't know anything about me?"

Sorin shook his head. "I've already told you that I don't. Why is it you have such trouble believing me?"

"Because it makes no sense! Why would you—why would anyone, but especially *you*—care about someone like me?"

"I don't understand. Why should I not care? What is it that's upsetting you?" Sorin's voice had grown louder too, but he looked more upset than angry.

Kaidyn exhaled tightly, trying and failing to compose himself. *I might as well just say it plainly.* As repugnant as it would no doubt be to Sorin, the noble obviously needed things spelled out for him. "Because, *Lord* Sorin, a man of your status has no business being concerned for a person of my background. Someone with Iskandir blood in his veins."

There was a brief silence as Sorin studied him carefully. Kaidyn struggled to maintain his control. Despite himself, he was rattled. He felt like he was embarrassing himself and probably Sorin as well, but sometimes it was better to have it out. Better to court disaster than have it find you.

" . . . You're Iskandir-born?" asked Sorin finally. His tone was devoid of any particular emotion.

"Half," said Kaidyn almost defiantly. "My father was born and raised in Iskandir. He could be dead now, for all I know. And my mother is the current ruler of Sareen, Queen Fianah Riverveil."

Another silence, broken only by the sounds of birds chirping outside and the more distant clashing of swords from one of the training halls. "Oh," Sorin said eventually.

"*Oh?*"

Sorin gave a little laugh, sounding unsure. "I don't know

what else it is you wish me to say," he admitted. "Should I be surprised? Troubled? Offended?"

"You . . . I can't believe . . ." Kaidyn fought to find the words and failed.

"In truth, I suppose I did not give your heritage any great thought one way or the other," Sorin broke in, seeing his reaction. "Does it matter so much to you?" He appeared genuinely curious.

Kaidyn's barely-held composure finally snapped. "Of course it matters!" he shouted, and saw Sorin's eyes widen. The healer took a step back.

Kaidyn lowered his voice again, but he was by no means finished. He was suddenly seething. His old anger tasted sour in his mouth and in his gut. He couldn't seem to rein it back in, now that it had been set loose again.

"Of course it matters," he repeated in a low hiss. "Do you know how many people would have happily left me lying there on the street to rot? How many would have been *glad* to see it? Just because of my father's blood? *Do you know how much that blood has cost me?*"

Sorin had paled. Far from looking disgusted or frightened, however, his features had taken on a grave sorrow. "I *don't* know," he said quietly, casting his gaze down. "I can't pretend to truly understand how you feel. But for what it's worth, I am sorry." He met Kaidyn's eyes again and looked at him steadily, making no attempt to mask his grief.

Kaidyn didn't know what to do or say to this. His customary response to anyone attempting to sympathize with his plight was to leave as quickly as he could, lest he lose any shred of self-control and do something irreversible. He had no time for empty platitudes, or for people who pretended to understand him when they obviously could not.

Most often, people did not even want to try—not really. They were hypocrites, concerned with their image and little more, and Kaidyn hated them with an anger that burned everything else in its path, deservedly or not.

At least, he had up until now. *Is it possible that Sorin means every word?* Had he somehow stumbled upon the one nobleman in the entire kingdom who would readily confess to not understanding and then apologize for it in the same breath?

The anger was suddenly gone, replaced now by something else — or maybe Kaidyn had only mistaken it for anger all along. The desire to be comforted gripped Kaidyn with a strength which not only surprised him, but shook him down to his very bones. He trembled as he took a step forward, then another, narrowing their distance to little more than a sigh. His hand stopped in mid-air, suspended in the act of alighting on Sorin's cheek.

More than anything, he wanted to touch this man. He had wanted to caress Sorin's face or run his fingers through his hair from the moment he woke up on his bed. No, he wanted to do even more than that. He wanted to hold Sorin, to draw him in close and provide him some measure of solace. Kaidyn could tell that Sorin's sympathetic expression was real, yet he couldn't find a logical explanation for it to be there. There was no reason for Sorin to care, but he did anyway.

But Kaidyn could not quite bring himself to invade that tiny space left gaping between them. He couldn't do it — not to Sorin, who so plainly deserved someone better. *He should have someone as true as himself, someone not weighted down by blind anger. I could never make Sorin happy. I would dirty him simply by trying.*

They stared at each other, unblinking in the afternoon rays of sunlight. It had grown perfectly still, the very air seeming to wait, motionless and anticipating something. Kaidyn stared at the reflection of himself in Sorin's eyes, standing frozen and afraid in front of him.

And then it was Sorin who was moving, slowly as though Kaidyn was a skittish animal, gradually dispelling the barrier between them until his fingertips finally came to rest, feather-light, over Kaidyn's heart. "If I could, I would heal this pain, no matter what it cost me," he said, and his eyes were wide and gazing at him almost giddily, as though he too felt off-balance.

Kaidyn could not tell which of them leaned forward first, closing the last inch still dividing them in the space of another breath, but his eyes slipped closed as their mouths met. Sorin's lips were cool and firm as well as warm and yielding. The kiss pulled him gently down until Kaidyn wanted to drown in it.

It was, despite this, almost chaste at first, because Kaidyn could not bear to be the one to abandon all thought of flight, and because Sorin seemed a little unsure of himself. But Kaidyn could not stop his hands from coming to rest almost possessively on the healer's sharp shoulders, and this was apparently all that was needed for reassurance.

Sorin parted his lips and dived deeper into the kiss as soon as Kaidyn's hand landed on his shoulders. It was as though he thought Kaidyn might disappear if he did not, and Kaidyn reached up further to run his fingers down Sorin's neck. In response, Sorin twined his fingers through Kaidyn's hair, tugging lightly and sighing into his mouth.

Kaidyn's hands fumbled with the top buttons of Sorin's shirt. *Gods, are we really doing this here, now?* But Sorin made no move to stop him, instead sliding wordlessly closer to the warmth radiating from the other's body. It didn't matter that they had only known each other for a matter of hours. It didn't matter that they were all but devouring one another in broad daylight in the middle of the infirmary.

Nothing and nobody mattered but them. Sorin pressed against Kaidyn's chest, making little noises of encouragement. Kaidyn's nails grazed Sorin's collarbone as the shirt slipped further down, revealing his shoulders. Meanwhile, Sorin's hand moved from Kaidyn's hair to cup his face.

Then Kaidyn paused, recognizing the feel of a ring against his cheek. He had not noticed Sorin wearing any jewelry on their first meeting, and pulled away to look.

It was a plain wooden ring, unexceptional in and of itself. There were no precious stones embedded in the wood, or even any kind of carving to decorate it. The light brown color might have been equally unexceptional, save for the faintly glowing veins of a much lighter shade running through it, almost white against the rest of the grain.

For all its lack of adornment, this was no mere market trinket. Anyone in the kingdom with even the faintest claim to established nobility, or any historian, would have immediately recognized it for what it was.

"Oh no, oh gods no," he said unthinkingly, and not even that kiss could prevent the shock from bleeding all warmth from him. "You're Sorin Silverwoods."

He saw Sorin flinch back at his words, or perhaps at the way in which Kaidyn spoke them, eyes now open wide and staring at him with . . . what was it Kaidyn saw there? Apprehension? Fear?

"Ahem."

They both started and turned in the same moment to where Nora stood in the doorway, her expression unreadable.

"I . . ." Sorin flushed, the red spreading all the way from the exposed top of his chest to the tips of his ears, and scrambled to re-button his shirt. He looked as embarrassed as if he had been caught completely naked, glancing between Nora and Kaidyn like he thought he might be reprimanded for his actions. Like *he* was the one who ought to feel ashamed.

"We weren't — that is, it was only — I didn't mean to —"

Kaidyn stepped forward, about to reassure him, to defend his honor if necessary, but it was too late. Flashing Kaidyn a last, panicked glance, Sorin lowered his eyes and brushed quickly past Nora, all but fleeing the room.

Though he did not know her well, Kaidyn liked Nora. She had the same measure of authority as any of the instructors within the academy, but like Kaidyn, she had no time for the games of the aristocracy, so she was therefore one of the few people in the school he truly respected.

Moreover, although Kaidyn had never heard her raise her voice even once, Nora was one of the most intimidating people he had ever known. He also knew her to be a highly competent and experienced physicker, as skilled in the more mundane aspects of healing as she was in her Gift. Briskly efficient in manner, Nora was whipcord thin and tall as a man. Her neat, almost delicate features made her seem young, even fragile to anyone who did not know better. Despite appearances, however, Nora was his senior by at least ten years, and while her touch was gentle enough, nobody was ever left in any doubt that the infirmary was her domain. Kaidyn had known her face since childhood, when she had been newly appointed Court Healer and little more than a girl herself, and still he trod carefully around her.

Currently, the woman in question was folding her arms and regarding him with an expression which was not quite a glare, but made Kaidyn instinctively nervous anyway and itching to reach for a sword he did not possess. Curiosity alone made him stand his ground. Judging by the conversation he had overheard the previous day, Nora seemed to be not only on familiar terms with Sorin but also related by blood, and Kaidyn could not pass up the opportunity to find out more when it was quite literally staring him in the face.

"Mistress Nora." He greeted her as calmly as he was able under the circumstances.

"Lord Riverveil." There was an undercurrent of sarcasm to her tone, but she did not sound angry. On the contrary, Nora appeared completely composed. "I gather you and Sorin are already . . . acquainted."

"I apologize if we caused a disturbance," he said, remembering the way he had shouted.

"We all lose our cool every now and then." Nora shrugged. "Some more than others, perhaps."

Kaidyn didn't know how to reply to that. He settled for a vague noise of agreement, prompting Nora to give an exasperated huff. "You lash out so easily because you keep too much to yourself," she clarified. "It's not healthy for the body, to say nothing of the mind. You would do better to find an appropriate way to channel it outwards — *not* that yelling is an ideal approach, of course." She raised an eyebrow, clearly waiting for some kind of verbal response this time.

Kaidyn cleared his throat. He was not embarrassed to have been caught being intimate with another man — such things were hardly uncommon — but he was embarrassed to have been caught with *Sorin*. Apart from their almost laughable difference in status, the noble did not deserve to have his reputation tarnished, and Kaidyn now felt honor-bound to defend it. "Whatever you think you saw — "

"Please." Nora held up a hand, stopping him. "You kissed him. Or he kissed you. Either way, I saw enough to know there's something between you, and likely more than just sex. *Not* that I think there's anything wrong in that," she said sharply as she saw Kaidyn about to interrupt.

"You . . . you don't?"

"Do I look like the kind of person who cares anything for the silly status games of court? I may be appointed by the queen, but there's a good reason I choose to spend most of my time here rather than up at the palace. And there's no need to look so astounded, Lord Riverveil. I don't own your body. You may do as you please with it. And to be perfectly frank, I couldn't be less interested in your bloodline if I tried."

It was easy to forget that she was a member of the gentry herself. Nora was direct to the point of bluntness and rarely displayed any of the traits Kaidyn associated with the nobility, but he still could not help but be taken aback by her casual attitude toward his actions. "Sor . . . that is, Lord Silverwoods fascinates me," he admitted, watching her expression.

Nora didn't appear startled. "Found that out, did you? Well, I'm not really surprised. It would have come to light eventually, and I told Sorin so. Several times, in fact."

"I don't understand. Why go to the trouble of hiding it?"

Nora gave him a forthright look. "I would expect you, of all people, to understand the need for a little privacy. Sorin doesn't like to be gawked at or thought of as some exotic animal, and I can't say I blame him."

"But why the embarrassment? It's as if he's almost ashamed of who he is."

"Ah. Like a certain other man we both know?" Nora met Kaidyn's gaze until he looked away, guilt tugging at him, before Nora sighed and seemed to take pity.

"Kaidyn, I like you. You're too stubborn and too proud by half, and you act like the entire world is against you, but I like you. You're a strong man and a good one, even if you're also a prize fool. Sorin is young and inexperienced. He's new to the capital and he wants above all to make a difference.

"How do you think it feels, to focus solely on honing one's abilities in order to help people, only to be constantly judged based on a name? If that sounds at all familiar to you, it should. Only unlike you, Sorin has even less choice about how he must comport himself among society."

Realization filled Kaidyn, quickly followed by a hot flood of shame. The Silverwoods weren't just aristocrats. They were one of the kingdom's three Great Families, and they were *old*—much older than the Riverveils, or even the Woodharts far to the south.

All Sorin had wanted was to be treated by Kaidyn as an equal, and he had not only refused to do so but thrown his nobility back in his face. If Kaidyn truly had the desire to do so, he could at least run away and start a new life for himself somewhere, far from court and free of all responsibility, for he had no role he was obligated to fulfill. Sorin, a powerful Gifted and the direct descendent of one of the kingdom's most important families, would never have that chance.

How could Kaidyn have been so *stupid*?

"If you understand, then I suggest you try to make it up to him," Nora suggested, accurately reading Kaidyn's silence. "He will forgive you—and probably more easily than he should, at that."

There was a note of unaccustomed fondness in her voice, but Kaidyn had more on his mind now than this. "Then answer me another question," he said. "Sorin's afraid of something, I know it. Something that has nothing to do with his name. What is it that he's running from?"

"That, Lord Riverveil, is not my secret to tell," she said, voice cool again, and Kaidyn knew very well he would get nothing more from her. He turned to leave.

"Kaidyn." Nora stopped him before he could exit the room, abandoning all formality. "Sorin may be only a distant cousin, but he is also a friend. We've known each other a long time. I don't know what it is between you two and I don't care. It's none of my business and besides, I think it will do you good. *Both* of you," she added, the ghost of a smile crossing her face.

"But I will say this . . ." All trace of humor vanished, the look in her eyes changing from gentle to terrifying in an instant. "If you ever hurt him like that again, even once, the gods themselves will not save you from me." She looked at Kaidyn unblinkingly, and it was with a supreme effort that he did not squirm under her gaze. "Do I make myself clear?"

Kaidyn's muscles twitched as his survival instincts kicked back in with a vengeance. "Yes, Mistress Nora."

CHAPTER FIVE

Kaidyn dreamed that night, unsurprisingly, of Sorin.
He became aware it was a dream the moment it began,
for the intensity with which he saw, heard, and felt things
could never have belonged to reality. It was as if all of his
senses had been impossibly, almost painfully, heightened.

*"Kai!" Sorin cried out and arched beneath him, his lean form
bared to Kaidyn's gaze. Their stomachs, hips, and thighs brushed
and rubbed against one another. Sorin moaned unashamedly as
Kaidyn bent down to kiss him, long and hard as though he hadn't
had the chance to do earlier that day, eagerly making up for his
mistake.*

"Sorin . . . I'm sorry. I'm so sorry. I never meant to hurt you."

*Sorin looked up at Kaidyn from where he was lying on the
ground, dazed. "I forgive you. Everything," he said breathlessly. "I
forgive you. So please, whatever you do, please just don't stop . . .
ahh, that!"*

*He writhed again in unfeigned pleasure as Kaidyn's fingers ran
through loose black hair. His fingertips landed softly on Sorin's
chest, mapping the lines of his body as it sloped smoothly down to
his stomach, past his naval, then dipped lower. The fingers were
followed by Kaidyn's mouth and tongue. He licked and sometimes
nipped lightly, loving the way Sorin twisted and shivered at his
attentions.*

*"You are beautiful," Kaidyn told him honestly before claiming
his mouth again, bearing down on already kiss-swollen lips. His
hand stroked between Sorin's legs, and Sorin gasped and threw his
head back, hair falling to reveal a pale neck that made Kaidyn at*

once want to mark it. It shook him, just how much he wanted that.

Then Sorin sat up, his gaze boring into Kaidyn's as he gripped him by the shoulders. He gently pushed Kaidyn until their positions were reversed.

Kaidyn was now lying on his back with Sorin leaning over him. Then, just as he had in the infirmary, the healer placed his hand over Kaidyn's heart—only this time there was no fabric to separate the touch, and the wooden ring Sorin wore felt warm against Kaidyn's skin, making Kaidyn's heart stutter in response.

"Shh. Can't you feel it?" Sorin whispered, and Kaidyn was about to answer him—of course I can—when Sorin gave another gasp and cried out again, this time not in pleasure but in agony as he clutched at his head.

"Sorin? What's wrong? Sorin!"

"It hurts! Oh gods, Kai, make it stop. Please make it stop, I don't want—" The words were cut off as Sorin went limp in his arms.

Kaidyn shook him frantically. "Sorin! Sorin, listen to me! You have to come back!"

"Kaidyn Riverveil." It was Sorin and yet also not. His tone was devoid of expression, a doll speaking with Sorin's voice. "Do you know what you have wrought?"

"What are you talking about? Where's Sorin? Give him back!"

"I am Sorin. He is me. We are the same."

"You're lying!"

Sorin continued as though Kaidyn had not spoken at all. "And you will be the one responsible for our death."

"Stop it!"

"Though you will not do so willingly, you will kill us."

Kaidyn recoiled, scrambling to get away from the words spoken with such eerie calm. Sorin's eyes cleared as soon as Kaidyn released him. He gaped at Kaidyn, the fear and horror plain on his face.

"Kai, no, don't leave me behind!"

"Never! I swear it." Kaidyn immediately reached out to grasp

him again—to draw Sorin in close and protect him from this . . . this whatever it was that tried to cause him harm, and to reassure them both that they were all right.

But in the brief moment they had been apart, an invisible barrier was thrown up between them. Kaidyn pounded at it with his fists, then hurled his whole body against it when it refused to give. He tried to break through it again and again as Sorin called to him from the other side, his voice gradually becoming fainter. Something was sapping at his strength and he was growing paler . . . no, his entire body was disappearing, gradually fading away into the very air.

"Kai! Kai, come back!" Sorin called, though this made no sense when it was he who was leaving Kaidyn. "Come back . . . don't go, please . . . please don't leave me alone, not now . . ."

"Sorin!"

But it was too late, far too late to do anything, and now the barrier was actively pushing Kaidyn further away, Sorin growing smaller and smaller in his vision as the gap between them widened. He tried to push back against it, to fight his way back to Sorin so that he could grab hold of him, but now something silent and powerful had Kaidyn in its clutches. He couldn't move, no matter how he struggled to free himself. Finally, Sorin was no longer even a dark speck in the distance. His voice, barely discernible now, sounded desperate and terrified.

"Don't . . . go . . . Kai!"

Kaidyn shot up with a jerk in his bed with the blankets strewn around him, shuddering. His muscles convulsed as they tried to chase after a phantom Sorin. He ran violently-shaking fingers through his hair, feeling the sweat already cooling on his brow and knowing with a terrible conviction that the nightmare had been more than just a dream. *But what? What?*

After a time, when he felt he could trust himself to walk, Kaidyn left the bed and stumbled to the window, where he stood looking out at the inky stillness. It was vast as a desert and just as desolate. His head ached and the stagnant heat of the summer air lay heavy in the close confines of his bed-chamber, yet he could not stop shivering.

There were still several hours until dawn. He knew he would not sleep again soon—and he was right. Kaidyn tossed and turned for the rest of the night, lying in the dark with only his thoughts for company.

At the first streaks of gray to permeate the gloom, he rose, dressed, and made his way to one of the several indoor training halls located within the school. The world was quiet and unmoving, and he knew it would be at least another hour before any activity began for the day. He felt closed in and suffocated, and was struck with the urgent impulse to *do* something—anything, so long as it involved getting up and moving.

This feeling was no stranger to him. Playing truant from the academy was not just a way of demonstrating his disdain at being forced to live and train in close quarters with men who openly despised him, and whom he despised in return. Neither was it merely a means of irritating his instructors, all of whom Kaidyn both disliked and distrusted. Rather, his escape from the school was just that—an escape.

When his own resentment grew so thick that he could taste it at the back of his throat, when the very walls seemed to make his skin crawl, then there finally seemed no choice but to seek a temporary reprieve—from his physical surroundings if nothing else.

And so, before morning had fully dawned, Kaidyn sought out the only space in which he could let his frustrations loose. With no sneering onlookers and nobody to force him to hold his strength in check—keeping him from lashing out too violently—Kaidyn was free for the moment to train as hard as he wished.

His boots echoed in the empty hall, floorboards squeaking a little as he crossed the room to remove one of the wooden practice swords from its resting place. It lay in his palm, a familiar and reassuring weight. It *belonged*. Kaidyn might have been unGifted and unable to lay claim to an unblemished bloodline, but his skill with the sword was true. Here, at last, was something he could take pride in.

He could already feel his stance changing as he held the sword, back straightening and shoulders losing some of their tension. His grip was strong and sure, yet not over-tight, as he readied himself and swung the sword in an arc that cut through the air, the motion smooth and free of uncertainty. Kaidyn's muscles easily bore the weight, and there was nothing and nobody to stop him from moving faster, swinging harder, turning more furiously to parry with an imaginary assailant. No scorn. No antipathy. He felt his body growing attuned to the weapon, letting him wield it gracefully. His sword was honest and cared for nothing at all beyond his own physical capabilities. It was something that he could grasp in his hand and know it to be real beyond any doubt.

So singular was Kaidyn's focus, his body beginning to ache pleasurably as the sword whistled through the air, that he did not notice anything else until he heard the sound of footsteps approaching. He jerked to a stop, his concentration shattering at the intrusion into his solitude.

"I'm so sorry, I didn't mean . . ."

Kaidyn could only stare.

Sorin swallowed, looking down before meeting his gaze again more steadily. "My Lord Riverveil," he began formally. "I did not mean to disturb you. I came here only to apologize for my actions yesterday. I had no intention . . ." He faltered, biting his lip.

Kaidyn saw that Sorin had also slept poorly, if at all. He looked wan, the marks of exhaustion heavy and pronounced. There was an air of fragility about him, as if he was holding himself together through sheer effort of will.

"I was too forward. I will treat you as I would any other person under my care, if that is your wish."

Kaidyn had not realized just how much it hurt to be held at arm's length. Having Sorin standing before him and speaking to him with such reserve made him see first-hand how much he must have wounded the nobleman. Nora needn't have warned Kaidyn against causing Sorin any further pain, for he could see all too clearly what he had done and was determined never to repeat it.

He dropped his sword. It clattered to the ground beside him, nothing but a lifeless piece of wood once more. "No. I'm the one who should be apologizing to you. I was wrong."

" . . . Kai?" The word was spoken hesitantly.

Kaidyn smiled, regret and self-loathing tinged with relief at being addressed by his name once more. "I hurt you. I thought to keep you at a distance — that I was doing right by pushing you away when I was only being careless. And I'm sorry for it."

Sorin gaped. "Kai, no . . .I didn't mean for you to — "

"I don't expect your forgiveness," Kaidyn broke in quickly. He needed to make himself clear while he still had the chance. "I only wanted to ask — to implore — that you allow me to make it up to you, in any way you see fit." He took a step forward, then another, slowly closing the distance between them of his own volition this time. "Anything." Willingly exposing his insecurities. Trusting Sorin with them in a way he had not done with a single person since he had grown out of boyhood, after he became too afraid to bare himself so completely to another. "Please," he pleaded, awaiting Sorin's judgment.

A small part of Kaidyn expected Sorin to reject him. He would do so politely, because he was nothing if not kind, but now that Sorin finally understood the depth of Kaidyn's vulnerability, he would cast Kaidyn's mistaken openness and desire aside. He would find someone infinitely more suited to bestow them on. Upon realizing who Kaidyn truly was, Sorin would no longer want anything more to do with him, and any further involvement on his part would be strictly professional.

The other part of Kaidyn—the part of him that could see the connection between them, however tenuous and indefinable, and had still chosen to tear down the walls—saw that Sorin had not yet turned away, and dared to hope.

"Truly, Kai? Anything?" Sorin's expression was serious, his voice grave as he too took a tentative step forward.

There could be only one answer, however much it scared Kaidyn to give it. He spoke it loud and clear into the gloom so that there could be no room for misunderstanding.

"Yes."

And then he could only try to breathe as Sorin, now with no hesitation whatsoever, moved into the circle of his arms. He looked up at Kaidyn, and there could be no mistaking his smile for anything other than simple joy.

"Then be with me."

Again, there was but one possible answer.

"*Yes.*"

For all its magnitude, it was not the only encounter Kaidyn would have in the same training hall that day.

The shadows were lengthening again when once more he found himself alone in the room, this time on his hands and knees as he polished the floor—another part of his ongoing punishment for his past infractions. He did not particularly care, for at least it allowed him to be alone and free to his thoughts. They had turned dark again now, his earlier elation from that morning having ebbed away as he realized he would have precious little time to spend with Sorin, no matter what they both might wish.

So long as they were returned by curfew, trainee officers regularly received dispensation to leave the academy grounds in order to visit relatives or attend court functions — such was their duty as young noblemen and courtiers. Kaidyn did not think he would be as fortunate. His official court duties were few indeed, and given his background, the instructors were doubtless disinclined to treat him with as much consideration as the other students, ensuring that any interaction he had with Sorin would be severely limited.

He had not had the chance to talk with Sorin about this. Sorin, who ate his meals alongside the trainees but unlike Nora did not remain for the night, had already returned to his townhouse. They had not had the chance to be alone again that day, though he never once left Kaidyn's mind.

Would Sorin already be asleep by now? Was he dreaming, and if so of what? Awake or lost to awareness, what thoughts troubled Sorin deep in the night, when darkness closed in around him? Yet again, Kaidyn recalled his dream from the previous night and shuddered. He did not know where it had come from, but hoped it was something he would soon be able to forget.

"Still not done?"

Kaidyn whirled around, though his face betrayed none of the shock of being intruded upon so suddenly. A fellow trainee, his face only vaguely familiar, stepped out of the shadows near the door, and Kaidyn inwardly cursed. He was hot and tired, certainly in no mood to return the inevitable insults. Kaidyn turned back to his task, ignoring the other man, hoping he would tire of his amusement quickly.

"I'm not here to mock you, you know," the other trainee continued. "I only came to see if you wanted some help finishing up."

Kaidyn was not interested in games. "I don't. Go away."

"I'm serious. It's getting dark and I know you haven't eaten yet. If we hurry you can still—"

"What part of *go away* was unclear to you?" The ruder Kaidyn was, the quicker he would probably be left alone.

"I'm only trying to help. Gods, are all of you this touchy?"

Kaidyn froze. The polishing brush dropped from his hands. "*What* did you just say to me?"

Clearly the other knew he had just uttered something he should not have, for he quickly took a step back at the note in Kaidyn's voice. "I didn't mean it to sound like that, all right?"

"Oh, I'm sure." Seething, Kaidyn got to his feet and turned to face his offender, already close to losing his temper. "Just like *all of you* don't mean it when you whisper insults under your breath or gossip like bored fishwives. If you have something to say, at least have the decency to do so to my face, and without a crowd of friends at your back to make you feel safer about it." He made no effort to hide his disdain.

"Look, I understand, all right? Some of us haven't exactly been welcoming. Though to be fair, it's not as if you've done a great job of getting to know any of us, either."

Kaidyn let out a scathing laugh at that. "I don't need to know you to see how you feel about me. You've made your position quite plain."

That earned him a scowl from the trainee. *Good.* Maybe the man would finally take the hint and leave him be. But the other soldier stood his ground. "Has it ever occurred to you that you're grouping us together in precisely the same way? You seem to think every nobleman in the city is jeering at you behind your back, each of us determined to hate you on sight. Not all of us are like that."

"Horse shit," Kaidyn spat. He was out of patience and had no intention of letting himself be taken in by whatever this man was playing at. The aristocracy used all manner of pretty words to try and hide their real motives, and Kaidyn had been seeing through them for years — this time was no exception. "Don't try to defend yourself to me or justify your actions when we both know exactly where you stand. I don't know what you think you have to gain from any of this, but people like you have no business suddenly trying to get in my good graces. Now leave."

"*People like me*? Do you even realize what you're saying?" When Kaidyn did not bother to reply, the other man's frown deepened. "You talk of injustice, yet here you are, judging me for having a title when you have no idea what kind of person I am. Do you even know my name?"

Kaidyn only laughed again scornfully. "Do you think I should have bothered to learn it when you have so patently little regard for me in return?"

The trainee finally lost his patience. "Emil," he said angrily. "My name is Emil. And I didn't come here for a fight, but since you're so obviously attempting to goad me into one . . ." He strode to the back of the hall and with no hesitation, retrieved two of the practice swords that were stacked against the wall. One of these he tossed to Kaidyn, who instinctively raised a hand to catch it. "Come on then. Since you seem so eager to fight anyway, let's have this out, here and now."

Kaidyn could not mask his disbelief. "You can't be serious."

Emil's only response was to hold his sword in the ready position.

"Private duels are strictly forbidden, in or outside the

academy."

"And you would never stoop to breaking any of the rules yourself, of course." The sarcasm was obvious.

It was enough to goad Kaidyn into positioning his own weapon to strike. "Fine." His fingers were already gripping the sword tightly. "But don't expect anything to come of this other than your defeat."

"Funny. I was about to say the very same."

But despite his words, Emil seemed in no rush to make the first move. And so, in the stillness that followed, Kaidyn gave no further warning but simply charged his opponent, determined to gain the upper hand from the outset. Emil should have been skilled enough to be able to defend himself in time, but in his anger, Kaidyn hoped to at least unnerve him.

What he did not expect was for Emil to strike ahead of him. His speed was admirable, and Kaidyn was forced to hastily block the attack, sword held horizontally across his body as Emil's caught it neatly in the center. The clattering of wood broke the quiet, and Kaidyn swung again before the sound had time to fade. This time it was Emil's turn to defend, and Kaidyn pressed the advantage, increasing his momentum and becoming more aggressive in his attacks, sure that he would eventually get beneath the other's guard.

But Kaidyn couldn't breech Emil's defense. To his surprise, the trainee blocked and parried every single one of his blows, grinning as Kaidyn tried and failed to land any of them properly. Clenching his jaw, Kaidyn moved faster still, raining down strike after strike and growing more frustrated with each passing moment.

Finally, breathing heavily, he was forced to move back, glowering at his opponent and searching for another opening while he struggled to regain his composure. In contrast, Emil looked only slightly out of breath and still quite calm, not even seeking to chase Kaidyn down but simply standing, watching. *Waiting.*

Infuriated more than he would have thought possible by this absence of reaction, Kaidyn snarled and rushed him again, determined that this time he should succeed. Again and again he failed, swinging and missing his mark until he felt himself tire. Sweating and cursing, aware that he was making a fool of himself, Kaidyn gritted his teeth and then struck hard and furious, deliberately holding nothing back. One more, just one more swing —

And just like that, his sword was flung through the air, spinning wildly from the force with which Emil had disarmed him. It landed with a sharp clatter several feet away, rolling across the floor until it finally came to a stop against the wall.

Silence fell again as Kaidyn recovered from his shock and exertion sufficiently enough to master himself, if only just, and walked with a pretense of calm to where his sword had been thrown. "A fluke," he said as casually as he could manage, his back still turned to Emil. "However, the next bout —"

"Enough of this," Emil interrupted him. "I know your style, I've seen you fight plenty of times before. You're good, but not nearly as good as you think you are. So know this — no matter how many bouts we fight, you will never be the victor."

Beyond anything else Emil had said or done this night, those words enraged Kaidyn. He spun to face him, naked fury on his face, but was not given the chance to spit out a response.

"Let me ask you something, Lord Kaidyn. And give me your honest answer. If you hate us so much, then why are you even here? You could be doing just about anything else, so why bother swinging a sword around so angrily in the first place?"

Kaidyn felt Emil was being mocking, purposefully taunting him with the title that everyone knew he did not have, and could barely voice his strangled reply. *"Why?"*

"It's not as though you're the only Half-Blood in this city. Iskandir and Sareen have been at each other's throats for years, but plenty of Half-Bloods have lived here since far before the war. Are you here to try and prove something on their behalf?"

Nobody had ever asked him such a thing. Struck dumb, he waited as Emil continued. "Or is it because you're unable to face your own blood and are fighting out of some kind of twisted self-hatred?"

"You — how dare you —"

"Because if that's the case, you'll lose to someone even halfway decent just like you did now, every time. Fighting with a bit of anger is one thing. But letting someone get to you so badly you can't even think? You won't make any kind of swordsman like that, let alone an officer."

"Come closer and say that again." Kaidyn had found his voice again and it emerged as a growl. He was shaking with rage, the sword trembling in his grasp. "Again, and you'll regret every word that came from your mouth this night."

Emil shrugged. "Only then you'd be little better than a thug. Thus proving my point, which you're smart enough to know. So I ask you again. Why are you here?"

And Kaidyn had no answer for him. None. There in the all but empty hall, the heat of the place and his own fury bearing down on him, Kaidyn could not reply — could do nothing but stand and stare like a fool as Emil strode over to place his sword back on its rail. When he reached the door, he stopped and turned back to Kaidyn over his shoulder.

"Let me know if you ever come up with an answer to my question. If you don't end up killing yourself first, that is."

He left then, abandoning Kaidyn to his thoughts and the encroaching shadows.

It was a long time before Kaidyn could force himself to face the growing darkness outside.

CHAPTER SIX

The next day, to Kaidyn's astonishment, he received permission to leave the academy after training was concluded each day, provided he returned by curfew. Caught off-guard, he didn't question the instructor who delivered the message. He assumed that Sorin must have interceded on his behalf, though he'd made no mention of this. As for his confrontation with Emil, the other trainee made no attempt to approach Kaidyn again outside of what was strictly necessary during combat exercises, though Kaidyn often thought he could feel the other man's eyes on him during these times. He ignored Emil's gaze and kept his distance. Beyond simply losing a fight, thinking of the encounter made Kaidyn profoundly uncomfortable, and he was determined to put it from his mind.

As the long, hot days continued to stretch out, Kaidyn instead focused all of his attention on taking advantage of his newfound freedom. Summer felt never-ending, but the warmth now seemed expansive rather than oppressive. Perhaps even he had not realized just how heavy his perceived imprisonment weighed on him until he was suddenly released from it. Even the time spent training at the academy was somehow more bearable now that he had something to look forward to at the end of it—something that was his and his alone.

The notion still made him giddy. Kaidyn half-felt he might at some point awake to find it had all been a fantasy brought on by the heat. He didn't know how else he could possibly begin to explain how he had stumbled upon such a person. It was as though Kaidyn had strayed into another world. When he told Sorin how he felt, the healer only smiled and said felt the same.

He spent his time learning Sorin—every lowered glance, every inch of skin, every inflection of his voice—and strangest of all, not minding in the least that he was being studied in return.

Though they were the same age, Sorin was in many ways Kaidyn's exact opposite. He was quick to smile, eager to please, and a stubborn idealist. Yet he still sought out Kaidyn's company day after day, not caring what anyone else might think. There was no pretense in him. Sorin's eyes might have been dark, but his laughter was bright, and this he gave away honestly and freely, expecting nothing in return.

Sorin also abhorred war, which struck Kaidyn as contradictory. In his way, Sorin was as much a part of the officer's academy as Kaidyn was, and if war with Iskandir continued then they would both be inevitably caught up in it. It was no secret that Sareen was fast running out of trained and able-bodied soldiers. Healers, meanwhile, were a growing rarity in the kingdom, and it was likely that Sorin himself would spend much of his time tending to the war-wounded once his own training was deemed complete.

"Sometimes war is necessary," Kaidyn told him once, and Sorin turned from where he had been lying on his side on the grassy bank to face him.

"But war is never *good*," he insisted. "No matter which side emerges the victor, everyone must always lose in the end." When Kaidyn frowned, trying to understand, Sorin continued earnestly. "We are the same, Kai. We have the same hopes and the same fears, Sareen and Iskandir. We both hope for peace and we both fear one another."

Kaidyn had never heard anyone else speak in such a way. "They're murderers! They would put all Gifted to the sword or the noose, convinced they're demons to be slain for the good of the world. Rumor has it the king's own younger son was forced to flee the capital. He's Gifted, and he had to run for his life, in fear of his own father!" The idea was distorted and unnatural to Kaidyn. It went against everything he had been brought up to believe.

"Doubtless they think the same of us. That we're murderers who would put a whole nation to the sword simply because we could. Meanwhile they see themselves as liberators, come to save our unGifted from the clutches of evil."

Kaidyn shook his head. UnGifted as he was himself, he had no wish to see his mother killed or dethroned, his sister slain, the whole kingdom ended. Iskandir's king was crazed and his kingdom had no mercy. Everybody knew this. "If they wanted to live in peace, they should have never provoked us in the first place," he protested. "They're the ones who started this war!"

"So it is said. Though I do wonder if that's the entirety of the story," Sorin mused.

"Then why do this? Why choose to help soldiers of all people if you're so opposed to what they — *we* — are doing?"

"Because," said Sorin, and his voice was light but his face was serious. "Somebody has to stop you from killing yourselves even as you try to save the rest of us." He raised an eyebrow then, propping his head on his hands so that he could look Kaidyn square in the eye. "Why are *you* here, of all people, when this kingdom treats you and your kind so ill? Even so, why fight for it?"

That came uncomfortably close to a certain other recent conversation, and Kaidyn still did not have an answer. He frowned and deflected the question with another. "You disapprove of fighting so much that you would not even defend yourself against personal attack?"

"Certainly I would," Sorin told him, still serious. "But I would never willingly harm another. Not if there were any other way." Then he brightened. "Of course, I am still a nobleman's son, trained in the use of a sword like any other." And to Kaidyn's surprise, Sorin grinned and leaped up, breaking off two long sticks from the dead trees near the riverbank to use as makeshift swords, teasing Kaidyn into sparring with him. Sorin was quicker than Kaidyn thought he would be, darting around his guard several times until his stick eventually snapped in two against Kaidyn's greater strength. Kaidyn sent them both tumbling, laughing breathlessly, to the ground, where he promptly stole a kiss. Sorin's lips tasted of fresh water and sunlight.

In the days and weeks that followed, Sorin worked hard in the infirmary, diligently attending to his craft and performing his duties with the utmost sincerity. There seemed to be nobody Sorin did not want to help. He insisted on studying not only the art of healing with his Gift but also the more commonplace methods of physicking—stitching wounds, setting bones, mixing herbs. For if ever this became necessary, Sorin explained, his hands must be ready to do what his Gift could not.

Still, Kaidyn noticed right away that Sorin loved to be outside. He did not fear his skin becoming darker in the sun but unconsciously tilted his face toward the sky, sighing happily whenever they left the confines of the training school. The pair often found themselves by a secluded part of the river bank as the shadows lengthened, removing their boots and rolling up their trousers to dandle their feet in the water, or else simply reclining in the dappled shade of the trees.

Both men preferred this to the bustle of the town. Kaidyn had long since developed a distaste for the suffocating press of bodies and invasive, never-ceasing noise of it, while Sorin disliked being stared at. His family's name, the oldest in the kingdom, had not remained a secret for long. While not precisely shy—Sorin was not loud but never afraid to speak his mind—it was obvious he did not enjoy undue attention. He often came and left the academy cloaked and hooded against prying eyes. Since many townspeople covered themselves in similar fashion, keeping the heat from their faces or their skin from darkening, this went largely unremarked. Kaidyn, who knew all too well what uninvited interest felt like, could not blame him.

Neither was Sorin timid when it came to showing his affection. He was a tactile person who apparently enjoyed exploring Kaidyn's body just as much as Kaidyn enjoyed exploring his.

Kaidyn did not normally like to be touched by others. The awareness of another's hands upon him was mostly an unwelcome and intrusive sensation. His past affairs, always with other men, had therefore been brief, both physically and romantically. But Sorin was different. He ran the tips of his fingers over the planes of Kaidyn's body, as unabashedly curious as a child but never seeming to push. He followed the contours of Kaidyn's form with his hands, tracing every ridge and crevice with soft, inquisitive strokes. He dropped butterfly kisses onto each of Kaidyn's scars—nearly all childhood accidents from roughhousing with Luck—and then responded with obvious pleasure when Kaidyn kissed him hungrily in return.

Sorin protested whenever Kaidyn complimented him or called him beautiful, instead claiming envy at Kaidyn's berry-red hair, his amber eyes and golden-brown skin—but had no qualms at all when it came to sex. This puzzled Kaidyn at first, for he had thought Sorin would be bashful when it came to physical intimacy, yet he was nothing of the sort.

Sorin laughed at him when Kaidyn finally brought up the subject. "What did you expect?" he said. "Kai, I might still be in training, but as a healer I can practically guarantee, there is nothing you can possibly possess that I've not seen before."

"Yet you blushed at our first meeting when I asked for my clothes back, having slept naked in your bed," Kaidyn pointed out.

Sorin flushed a little. "Ah. But you were my patient then, my responsibility. I should not have been thinking of you as . . . well. I thought you very handsome," he replied. And Kaidyn had to work very hard at not ravishing Sorin where they lay, in broad daylight for all to see should someone happen to pass by.

There was another oddity. Kaidyn had seen Sorin naked in light and in darkness, but had seen no sign of any tattoo. He was Gifted, yet bore no mark of such, though tattoos were proudly etched into the skin of every other Gifted Kaidyn knew. Ladies often wore them on the inside of their wrists so that they could coyly show them off as they fanned themselves or made a pretense of adjusting billowing sleeves, and many men could be just as preening.

"Neither of my siblings have their tattoos either," Sorin admitted when Kaidyn asked him about this. "My older brother came late to his Gift, and by then I had already decided that if he did not have one, neither would I."

"What of your sister?" Kaidyn asked, knowing the pains many women went to, flaunting their tattoos like expensive jewels.

"Alora is unGifted."

"Oh." Kaidyn sat up a little. "Is that . . . does your family..?"

"I think we're all a little glad of it," Sorin said, smiling faintly. "Don't look so shocked, Kai. Of course, Alora is young still, only a child yet, and it may come to her in time. But Gifts can be more trouble than they're worth, especially when it comes to children. Control often comes with difficulty. Doubtless my parents were glad of the respite."

Kaidyn had never heard anyone speak of being Gifted in such terms. "But Gifts are . . . they're something to be proud of," Kaidyn protested. "They help people, they . . ." He trailed off, thinking of the countless times he'd heard it praised, how he and Lyrah had shared their envy of the Gifted as children, but Sorin shook his head.

"They do help people, and not a day goes by when I'm not happy to be a healer. This will be my life's work, and for that I can be proud. But Gifts can be dangerous too, much like a weapon if put into the wrong hands. Would you carelessly hand a sword to a child? What of a tyrant or a madman?"

"The use of a sword is a skill," Kaidyn countered. "A Gift is inherent."

"Gifts must be trained too, lest they do more harm than good. Come now, surely you've read such stories as well. The histories are rife with tales of Gifts gone tragically wrong. And Gifts are not all-powerful, either," he continued when the royal made to argue. "They say that every talented weather-Gifted in the kingdom has been summoned to the palace, yet still there's been not a drop of rain in months. Sareen can ill-afford a drought." And to that Kaidyn had no retort.

They spoke of everything and nothing as the summer continued, Kaidyn recounting some of the trouble he'd gotten into with Luck, Sorin talking of his own childhood — according to him, much of it spent climbing trees, swimming in the river, and hiding from his teachers.

"Mischievousness runs in the family, or so I'm told," Sorin told him, and Kaidyn could well believe it now. Sorin was all sober concentration as he worked, but shed this side of himself like a cloak whenever he was alone with Kaidyn.

They took turns swapping secrets — some big, others laughably small.

"I used to be terrified of horses," Sorin told him furtively.

"And for years I wanted a tiny one as a pet, just so I could feed it apples and sugar lumps," Kaidyn returned.

"I wanted to be a pirate when I grew up."

"I imagine you'd look quite fetching in an eye patch," Kaidyn grinned. "I wanted to be a knight."

"Like Kaidyn the Brave?"

"Exactly like Kaidyn the Brave. I badgered my mother into reading me stories about him incessantly," he remembered. "I was so determined to slay my first dragon. She didn't have the heart to tell me they'd been extinct for over a century."

"A pity. I can well imagine you as a knight. Though with your hair and eye color, perhaps you are more dragon than slayer," Sorin grinned, then continued. "I escaped a lesson once by climbing out the window and onto the roof when my tutor's back was turned."

"I accidentally knocked over mother's favorite vase playing with Luck and hid the pieces under my pillow. She never did scold me for it when she found out."

"I played hide-and-seek with my brother, but left him hiding so that I could sneak outside to go swimming in the river during a rainstorm."

"I'm afraid my sister despises me." Kaidyn blinked. Where had *that* come from? He hadn't meant to say it, and he glanced quickly away as his vision unexpectedly blurred.

But his lover would have none of it, and Kaidyn allowed himself to be pulled close to Sorin's chest, his face turned so Sorin could bring their foreheads together until they softly bumped. "No. Ah no, my Kaidyn," Sorin whispered. "You are loved more than you know — of this I am certain."

After a while, when Kaidyn had mastered himself again and the fog before his eyes had cleared, Sorin wiped the last of the dampness from his face with gentle fingers.

"I know little enough of your family — only that which is common knowledge, I suppose. Your mother was an only child, yes? And your sister is your only sibling."

"That's right."

"What was your father like?"

"I don't know," Kaidyn replied. He was glad for something else to think about. "I was but three summers old when he left." He frowned, trying to remember, but all he could call to mind now was a flash of golden hair and eyes like his own. Both were details Kaidyn's mother had told him in the past, and for all he knew were not really true memories at all, only imaginings.

"Do you hate him?"

"What? No!" The idea was an alien one to Kaidyn, who had grown up hearing his mother talk of him in wistful sighs. "Father was . . . he didn't leave because he wanted to. Nobody ever talked of it — at least not to me — but when I eventually gathered the courage to ask, my mother admitted that she was the one who'd finally sent him away. This was common enough knowledge among the court. War had not yet broken out, but nobody approved of her taking a lover from Iskandir, let alone actually marrying him. And not even a noble or a swordsman at that, but a traveler-merchant. Such a match would never have been suitable, even had he been Sareen-born."

"Yet she married him anyway."

"She did." Kaidyn smiled. "My mother is well-loved, but she is stubborn in her way. Some call her contrary. She disregarded all who spoke out against it, even the Council. And when it became clear our treaties with Iskandir were about to fall apart, just as everyone had been saying for years they would . . ." He fell silent a moment, and Sorin waited.

"Then the pressure just became too much for them, I suppose. We were on the verge of war. When mother told him to go, my father had no choice. She was the Queen, and he only the Queen-Consort." Kaidyn shrugged. "Soon after that we left the northern palace for good and moved to the capital."

"What was his name?" Sorin asked after a moment.

"I never knew his family name. But his first name was Henri." Kaidyn had not spoken it in many years, and the word felt strange on his tongue. "Anyway," he continued when Sorin remained quiet, "this was all a long time ago now, though as Lyrah grew older I think she only became more aware of it. After a while she simply stopped talking to me, though we were close enough once. She is the heir, after all, and perhaps felt the loss of her own father more keenly than I did mine. Certainly she remembered her own father better." Kaidyn lay back, not sad now so much as reflective. "I can't even remember the last time she and I spoke."

"Did the queen love him? Her first husband?"

"I don't know." Kaidyn paused to consider. "She speaks of him fondly, though not I think with any great passion. It was a marriage of convenience, politically sound. And she was very young, still a child really. He was much older."

"And your mother never married again after Henri."

"No. She didn't." Kaidyn could not do other than smile at that, remembering the promise she had made to him one night, just before his eighth name day.

The smile did not go unnoticed. Sorin angled his head for a kiss, slow and deep and infinitely caring—and Kaidyn wondered if, in spite of the pain, a wound buried somewhere deep inside him was finally beginning to heal.

There was only one subject about which Sorin refused to

speak, and Kaidyn was sure this had something to do with the conversation he had overheard weeks earlier in the infirmary. If Sorin had spoken again about it with Nora, Kaidyn was not aware of it. Sometimes he saw another side of Sorin that worried him and had to remind himself not to pry. Gods knew he hated it when people tried to interfere with his own business, so Kaidyn was unwilling to force the issue. However much he longed to banish whatever was responsible for stealing that smile away, it was something they both left alone.

But more often their time was filled with shared laughter and shared touches, uninterrupted evenings marked by the lazy exploration of one another's bodies, and a bone-deep contentment that felt like it might never have to end.

Kaidyn thought he had never before known such peace.

Though nobody watching could fail to notice their growing closeness, Kaidyn and Sorin kept their relationship to themselves and in turn were largely left alone. However, at least one person made his displeasure apparent.

Kaidyn knew at the back of his mind that he had been neglecting Luck. They had scarcely met since their conversation just before Sorin's introduction to the school, and those meetings they had managed to snatch had been hurried and unsatisfactory. Kaidyn knew it was at least partly to do with Sorin, and that he owed Luck some kind of explanation, but as the days turned into weeks, he felt less and less inclined to talk about it. If Kaidyn had often been somewhat taciturn, he had never felt the desire to hide anything from Luck until now. The thought put a dampener on their increasingly sporadic time spent in one another's company. Worse was the fact that his earlier exploits with Luck, spent mostly drinking and half-purposefully getting into fights, now felt childish to Kaidyn, even tawdry.

He was aware he was not quite the same person he had once been. His fury and his wounded pride still waited to lash out, bitter and resentful beneath the surface of his newly discovered happiness, but it was as though this part of himself was presently slumbering. Kaidyn had no desire to wake it. Nonetheless, Luck was his friend and brother-in-arms. The cook's son had stood by Kaidyn when the world had seemed at its darkest, and he would never forget it.

It was in fact Sorin who encouraged him to seek Luck out once more. "It's not right that I should take up all of your time. Go to him, Kai. He cares for you deeply, as I know you do for him. And . . ."

"And?" Kaidyn prompted at Sorin's uncharacteristic hesitation.

" . . . And I think he will be very important to you, when the time comes," Sorin said, an odd ring to his voice. "He is connected to you and will yet have a vital role to play. Don't abandon him." Then he smiled, rubbing at his temple absentmindedly, and the strangeness vanished. "You should treasure your friends." And Kaidyn could hardly argue with that.

It was another hot evening, close and muggy, when Kaidyn searched for Luck and found him alone outside one of their frequented taverns. Luck's features appeared thinner, sharper, and there were marks that looked like fading bruises about his face. Still, he got up and clapped Kaidyn on the shoulder in welcome when he saw him. Kaidyn quickly offered to buy him another drink.

"It's been a while," Luck said, his gaze taking Kaidyn in once they sat with their ales. "I was worried they'd been pushing you too far in that fancy school of yours. Grinding you down."

"Never." They shared a knowing smile, knocking their tankards together.

"So," Luck lifted an eyebrow after a few thirsty gulps. "What news? Seems I've heard nothing from your neck of the woods in an age. Been keeping you under lock and key, I suppose?"

"Not exactly," Kaidyn hedged, wondering where to start. "You first, though. How is everyone doing?" Though he knew only a few by name, he felt far more of a connection to the others like himself than he did with the noblemen among whom he lived and trained.

Luck gave a careless shrug. "Same as always. As well as any of us can, living in a place like this. Better for us maybe if we weren't in the capital. We all know the war will be dragging out a while yet, maybe years, and who's to blame for it? We get that knocked into our skulls every day. Half-Blood, half enemy. But we do all right for ourselves. Knock back, when we have to."

"At the training school?"

"Elsewhere too," Luck grinned. "We manage, just like we always have."

"But nobody's being ill-treated?" He eyed Luck's bruises, but knew Luck would not thank him for asking how he'd come by them.

The question earned Kaidyn a snort. "I doubt that's a word anyone cares about anymore. Unlike your academy, we enlisted men get some pretty low-bred sorts, and half the instructors are barely better behaved. We fight when we must." Luck tossed back more of his ale and sank bank in his chair. "A few left," he added, almost as an afterthought. "Couldn't take it, I reckon."

"Left what?"

Luck shrugged. "The school. The city, if they're smart. Couldn't exactly ask them, could I? If word ever got out before they'd made their disappearance . . ."

Kaidyn sucked in a breath. Outside of battle or not, desertion was no light matter. "If they're caught—"

"I know. No lashing for them. They'll have to make what lives for themselves as they may elsewhere now. Take up as mercenaries, maybe, or else give up the sword altogether. Somewhere far enough away from the capital that they won't be recognized." He looked at Kaidyn thoughtfully, eyebrows raised. "What of you?"

Luck obviously did not wish to linger on the topic, and so Kaidyn smiled despite his misgivings. "Oh, they'll have to try harder if they want me to leave. Though there might have been a few fights," he said, and Luck laughed shortly.

"I'll bet. Though least you've probably got better food where you are. More of it, too."

Kaidyn wondered if Luck was getting enough, although he was well aware his friend would never say if it were otherwise. "Mm. They say the city is suffering a shortage. The drought." The war as well, though neither saw fit to mention that.

They continued to drink, talking of small and unimportant matters before the conversation finally turned toward what Kaidyn knew it must.

"Are you still friends with him?"

"Who?" Kaidyn asked though he knew perfectly well.

"Don't play dumb. That dashing rescuer of yours. What was his name?"

Now it was Luck who was pretending at ignorance. "Sorin."

"*Sorin*. Right."

Kaidyn took another sip, buying more time to think. "We're still friends. I told you he started work in the infirmary? It turns out that he and Nora are related, actually. Cousins, albeit distant ones."

"Yeah, you told me that already too."

"Yes, well. He's a strong healer, or so Nora says," Kaidyn

commented, searching for something else to say.

"You sure know how to pick 'em."

There was an uncomfortable pause as Luck stared into his tankard and Kaidyn fidgeted with his, wondering how to fill the silence. " . . . That's not all there is to him, either," he finally said.

"Go on, then."

Kaidyn took a breath. "His name is Sorin Silverwoods."

The look of surprise in response was almost comical. "As in *the* Silverwoods?"

"Who else is there?"

Luck's eyes glittered. "Interesting. And what does such a high-born lord want with you?"

"He doesn't want anything."

Luck snorted, leaning back in his seat. "Come now, you know as well as I they all want *something*. Money. Power. Certain choice favors?" He raised an eyebrow, the implications obvious. "You'd do well to steer clear of people like him."

Kaidyn tried not to let his annoyance show. "He's not like that. Sorin is . . . he's different."

"Different? Different how?"

"He . . . he just is, all right?" Kaidyn struggled to explain. "He's . . . I don't know how to say it. He's *real*, Luck. He's not like most nobles, he doesn't care for his name or his influence. You'd see it for yourself for in a moment if you met him."

"But I haven't," Luck pointed out, a sharp note to his voice. "And if you took a step back you'd probably be able to see the bigger picture for yourself."

Kaidyn frowned. "Meaning what, exactly?"

Luck held up his hands in a pacifying gesture. "Meaning, I know you two have been spending a lot of time together, that's all. I saw you passing through town the other day, though you didn't notice me. Too busy not keeping your hands to yourselves, is how it looked."

There was something other than the usual friendly teasing in the way Luck said this, and Kaidyn flushed, half-embarrassed to be caught out and half-irritated at his friend's attitude. He took another gulp of his drink, attempting to swallow down his temper along with it. "It's true we've been in each other's company a lot," he said after a moment. "But it's exactly because of this that I know who he really is, not in spite of it."

Luck placed his now-empty tankard down a little harder than necessary, wiping roughly at his mouth with the back of his hand. "It's not like you to be swayed by just a pretty face, Kai." He leaned back in his chair again when Kaidyn made no move to answer, surveying him carefully. "You're in love with him."

Kaidyn went still. "What?"

"You heard me. Yeah. It all makes sense now. Why you've been conveniently avoiding the rest of the world. How you can stand to have him touch you like that. You're in love with him. With *Sorin*."

"Don't say his name like that," Kaidyn said quietly.

"Like what?" Luck challenged.

"Like you hate him. Like you even know him enough to do so."

"Because you'd never do the same yourself when it came to any other noble? Besides, I already know more than enough. I know you've only been trying half-heartedly at best to meet me lately. I know you've had your head manipulated by a fancy lordling with a fancy name. I know you've fallen for the likes of someone just like the rest of them—shallow-minded and greedy. I'm surprised you can even—"

"Shut up," Kaidyn warned him.

But Luck refused to stop. "Don't tell me you haven't realized it for yourself. I bet he's laughing at you behind your back, just like everyone else is now. What happened to us against the world, huh? To telling them to shove their gods-be-damned rules and watching them destroy themselves with their own stuck-up arrogance? Now you're on *their* side?"

"I'm on nobody's side!"

"You used to be on mine!" Luck glared, the hurt and resentment plain on his face.

With a supreme effort, Kaidyn waited until his fists had unclenched before he spoke again. "That's not what I meant and you know it. It's just . . . I've come to see I was mistaken. It's not like we thought it was, Luck. It doesn't have to be us against them anymore. I don't like the balance of power any more than I did before, but not every single nobleman is the enemy. They didn't get a say in which family they were born to any more than we did, it's not fair to just—"

"Oh, I think I know very well what you *meant*," Luck spat. Disgust colored his tone. "But what you think and what you say are two different things, and they never were before. What the hell happened to you?"

"It's true, I won't deny it. I've changed. But before you say anything, know that it wasn't Sorin who changed me. I'm the one who chose to change myself."

"Oh, it was Sorin all right," Luck scoffed. "But you're right in one way. You *have* changed. You've become weak."

"Stop."

"Sorin's taken away your pride and all he's given you in return is a bleeding heart!"

"I said stop!"

"Is he really that good, Kai? Does he whisper sweet nothings in your ear when he lets you fuck him? Does he beg when you—"

Kaidyn's chair scraped across stone as he leaped up,

grabbing Luck by the front of his shirt. "I said, *enough*," he growled, low and furious. "Not a word more, or else . . ."

"Or else what?" Luck mocked him. "You going to finish that threat of yours? Will you sic your pretty little noble on me?" His eyes narrowed, voice lowering in a mockery of intimacy. "Does he use his teeth in bed same as you used to?"

Kaidyn stilled his hand with less than an inch to spare from Luck's jaw, and his friend grinned, hard and feral. "Do it, Kai. Prove you've got at least this much fight left in you. Well, what are you waiting for?" he prompted when Kaidyn didn't move. "*Do it!*"

They stared at each other, neither of them willing to back down, until at last Kaidyn uncurled his fingers, releasing his hand from where it had still been gripping a fistful of Luck's shirt. "I'm not going to hit you," he said finally, and took a deliberate step back.

"Then go back to your precious nobleman." Luck sneered. "At least you'll have the comfort of someone to warm your bed at night when the rest of us are finally sent off to die."

Kaidyn turned his back before his anger could surge up a second time, closing his eyes for a moment and allowing the words to wash over him. Without further comment, he began to walk away.

"If you're looking for your courage, you'll find it thrown by the wayside, along with your pride!" he heard Luck yell after him, but Kaidyn did not stop or turn to face him again.

And though he knew it was for the best, he ached for what had once been between them, and for something that, whatever Sorin had told him, Kaidyn felt was now lost forever.

CHAPTER SEVEN

Kaidyn suppressed a shiver.

Almost overnight, it seemed, the warmth of the sun had been replaced by a bitter breeze. It was clear the long summer was finally over. Very soon the first frosts would arrive. Kaidyn could already see his breath puffing out in white clouds in the early morning, and again in the evenings when the light began to wane ever more swiftly. Fall was short and sharp. The snows would perhaps fall early that year.

The thought of winter did not usually trouble Kaidyn. Outdoor training would continue unless especially heavy snow made it impossible, and he had never been bothered by the cold. Sorin was another matter. Kaidyn worried for him. Sorin stubbornly refused to employ live-in servants, and past experience with the aristocracy told Kaidyn that many a noble was incapable of even dressing themselves without assistance.

Sorin only laughed off Kaidyn's concerns. "But I don't need any servants," he always insisted. "I eat my meals alongside everyone else at the academy, and I'm perfectly capable of much of the rest myself. I might not be as worldly as you, but even I know enough to draw water and sweep a broom." He did, Sorin claimed, have a young boy from town who came to help him sometimes with cleaning and take his clothing to be laundered, among other small tasks, and Kaidyn believed him only because he knew Sorin was all but incapable of telling a lie.

And so the season passed, uneventful but for two things.

The first was an injury.

Sorin was alone in the infirmary when Kaidyn and one other trainee officer half-dragged, half-carried the screaming man between them inside. It was Emil.

"What happened?" asked Sorin urgently, already helping to lay the wounded soldier down on one of the made-up beds.

Kaidyn looked to the trainee who had witnessed the incident first-hand. "Fool green horse spooked and threw him right off," he grunted, trying to hold Emil still so that Sorin could examine him. "It's his leg. I think it's broken."

Kaidyn gripped Emil's right side, attempting to stop his thrashing. "Sorin, where's Nora?"

"She isn't here today. She's visiting the palace to help tend to some people there who have taken ill. I don't know how urgent it is, and it would take too long to fetch her back in any case. But . . . I don't know that I alone—"

"Sorin." Kaidyn spoke intently, seeing his doubt. Their gazes met over the bed. "You can do this. Nora would never have left you alone if she thought you weren't capable of handling things." He did not need to say that if Emil's leg could not be mended, he would likely never wield a sword professionally again. His life as an officer and a soldier would be over.

Sorin took a steadying breath and nodded, already moving to the front of the bed where he placed his hands just above Emil's head. His Gift shimmered and rippled, colorless but distorting the air as it blossomed out around his fingertips. Emil instantly calmed, his limbs ceasing in their jerking, and his groans fading to whimpers. "It's all right," Sorin soothed. "Emil, it's all right. I know you're in pain, but it will soon pass. Now, close your eyes and try to focus only on my voice, just breathe for me nice and slow . . . that's right, just like that, you're doing well . . ." Sorin's voice flowed on, low and comforting as Emil's eyes gradually closed, his movements stilling completely as he lapsed into unconsciousness. After a moment, Sorin's eyes closed as well. The current of air around him grew stronger as he concentrated, seeking out the source of the wound.

"You can let go now," he said, and it took Kaidyn and the other trainee a moment to realize he was directing his words at them. They released Emil, standing back from the bed.

If there was any more hesitation at not having Nora there to guide him, Sorin gave no outward sign of it.

"Do you want us to leave?" Kaidyn asked softly after a moment.

"Kai, will you stay?" Sorin opened his eyes to look at him, and Kaidyn saw no fear reflected back — only the desire to be kept company by someone he knew and trusted.

"Of course."

The other soldier who had helped carry Emil inside slipped quietly away when Kaidyn nodded to him.

"Do you need anything else?"

Sorin shook his head. "Only time. I do not know if I can mend the bone. Not by myself. The break isn't clean, there are fragments . . ." He trailed off, biting his lip again before squaring his shoulders. "But he's bleeding on the inside, and I've no choice but to try. Will you make sure the room stays quiet, please?"

"Of course," said Kaidyn again, and briefly touched Sorin's hand. "I know you can do this."

Sorin favored him with a fleeting smile. "With you by my side, how could I not believe?" he murmured, almost to himself. He pulled a nearby chair closer and seated himself by the side of the bed, leaning over the injured soldier. But for the starkness of Emil's pallor and the fact that he had been screaming mere moments earlier, he might have only been sleeping as normal. Sorin placed his hands over Emil's thigh, and the room fell silent.

Kaidyn could do little to help. He got up once to whisper to one of the school's instructors who appeared at the infirmary door, but was otherwise unable to do anything except watch, hoping his presence was in some way reassuring. Sorin's face was tranquil as he worked, almost as though he too had simply nodded off in his chair but for the occasional movements of his hands.

Kaidyn tried to imagine what it would be like, envisioning jagged pieces of bone scattered inside Emil's leg and Sorin trying to piece them back together like tiny shards of glass. He wondered what it felt like for Emil to have a stream of magic flowing through him as Kaidyn himself had when Sorin healed him months earlier. Had it been warm, or had it felt cool like water? He tried to remember if he had been aware of it, somewhere inside his unconsciousness. *Or is such magic impossible to sense?*

Trying to remember was like attempting to recollect a dream, with only the barest of impressions left over in his mind. His focus went back to Sorin, who continued to breathe steadily in and out, and after a while Kaidyn noticed that Emil had come to match him breath for breath.

There was no way of knowing how much time slipped past. Sorin was still silent and bent over Emil as though in prayer. At some point his hands had stilled, the scene becoming motionless enough that the two men could have been carved of stone were it not for the measured rise and fall of their chests. The light coming from outside of the window began to dim as day faded into evening.

Finally, just as Kaidyn was starting to worry in earnest, Sorin stirred. His head lifted tiredly, and he scrubbed a hand over his face before his eyes focused on his surroundings. "Kai..?" His voice sounded a little disorientated.

Kaidyn was by his side in an instant. "I'm here. Tell me what you need."

"Nothing. I think . . . I think it's done. What of Nora?"

"Not yet returned, but word was sent up to the palace. She shouldn't be far away," Kaidyn told him. He searched Sorin's face and saw the weariness there, and the cautious, unspoken relief.

Sorin stood, grimacing a little at the stiffness he no doubt felt from the hours of inactivity, and looked back down at the bed. "He should sleep another few hours at the least. Probably through the night. I won't know until then if everything is at it should be. And the bone and surrounding flesh may still be tender, fragile. But the worst of the damage is mended to the best of my ability."

"Nora would be proud of you," Kaidyn told him quietly. "*I* am proud of you."

Sorin looked up at him and offered a wan smile. He opened his mouth to reply — and his eyes slipped closed as he fell, senseless, into Kaidyn's arms.

The second thing to occur toward the end of that season was perhaps linked to this incident, although Kaidyn supposed nobody would ever be able to know for sure.

Emil's leg mended strong and true. Nora praised Sorin's skills when she examined the injury herself later, but she had frowned upon hearing of Sorin's collapse. "You give too much of yourself," she warned him. "Remember, our Gift is our own life force we spend. It can be replenished, but the more we offer, the higher the price." Kaidyn had not moved from Sorin's side even when he'd woken. He saw his lover look down now, dutifully embarrassed, though both student and teacher still seemed pleased at Emil's recovery.

Soon after this, however, as temperatures outside plummeted and the weather grew worse, sickness swept like a fire through the academy, and those unlucky enough to be caught in its wake burned, dizzy and delirious with fever.

Nora and Sorin worked hard to ease their suffering, and trainee soldiers were assigned to help by making beds, fetching extra blankets, and drawing water in turns, but the illness could not be stamped out so readily and the effort was clearly taxing. Not a single word of complaint passed Sorin's lips, but Kaidyn could see the exertion taking its toll.

"Is this normal?" Kaidyn asked Nora in a low voice as he brought over freshly dampened cloths for her.

"The illness is common enough around this season, and typically not serious if promptly treated," she replied, brisk as always and hands busy preparing a tincture. But then she conceded, "The symptoms are perhaps more severe and long-lasting than usual. We are lucky to have another healer on hand this time."

They both turned to glance at Sorin, who was speaking in an undertone to another patient and clasping his hand as the soldier slid into a fitful doze. Dark rings circled Sorin's eyes, but as soon as the man fell asleep, Sorin turned to another, ready to offer what comfort he could.

By the time the stream of patients to the infirmary finally began to slow days later, the strain on the academy's newest healer had become obvious. Nora ordered him to rest when he walked into the academy early one morning.

"I can't," he said, and Kaidyn, who with Nora's tacit approval had taken to helping Sorin personally, thought he looked ready to drop. Kaidyn did not know whether Sorin had fully recovered from healing Emil, or if the spread of sickness alone drained him so. However, he was not surprised to see Nora fold her arms at Sorin's protests.

"I can and will handle things alone today. You are to return home, and I expect Kaidyn to see you there without incident."

"But—"

"No. Enough, Sorin. You put your own health in jeopardy

by staying. Besides you're of no use to me ill. Go home."

Her words were harsh, but Kaidyn was glad of it. Sorin's jaw was slightly clenched, betraying his headache. Kaidyn also noted the slight tremble of his hands as he fumbled with his cloak, reluctantly accepting Nora's decision. But Sorin drew the line at allowing Kaidyn to escort him back to his townhouse.

"Stay with Nora, please," Sorin begged him. "She's exhausting herself as well, and you've been such a help these past few days."

"I don't think—"

"Please, Kai! I'll go straight home, I swear to it, but I trust you more than anyone to make sure Nora has whatever help she needs. I'll sleep as soon as I get back. You can visit me later today when things here have quietened."

Kaidyn hesitated, but Sorin squeezed his hand, entreating Kaidyn to grant his request. " . . . All right. I'll stay. But I *will* pay you a visit later," Kaidyn promised, and was rewarded with a smile.

Sorin finally left, issuing a rush of last-minute instructions before Kaidyn gently shushed him and sent him on his way. Nora kept Kaidyn and several other volunteers busy fetching and carrying for several hours, but he was unable to stop thinking about Sorin. He got ready to leave at the earliest opportunity and Nora shooed him out, her own concern not quite hidden well enough to fool him.

Nonetheless, it was already approaching dusk as Kaidyn made his way to Sorin's home, treading the path he now knew so well. The house was quiet when he arrived, and he could see no candle or lamplight from within. He knocked unobtrusively, then harder when he received no answer. Assuming Sorin was already sleeping, Kaidyn tried the door and found it unbarred, then made his way past the parlor and the small kitchen area. He nearly tripped over a body, lying still and cold on the unforgiving stone.

"Sorin!" Kaidyn groped for some candles and tinderbox and bent over his unconscious lover, who did not respond to his name. The light revealed he was lying face down on the floor, one arm slightly outstretched from where he had tried to break his fall. There was no blood, but Kaidyn's fingers discovered a bump on Sorin's head, and there was no telling how long he had been there on the cold stone or what had caused his collapse.

Once Kaidyn had assured himself that Sorin did not seem to be otherwise harmed, he carried him into the bedchamber. Sorin did not so much as twitch when his body was placed on the bed with the blankets securely around him.

There was no sign of a fever, and his breathing seemed normal. Kaidyn thought about running to fetch Nora, but loathed the thought of leaving Sorin alone. He settled for lying beside him on the bed, pulling him close to warm him more quickly. Then, heart pounding his disquiet, Kaidyn waited.

When Sorin finally stirred, Kaidyn's burst of relief turned to alarm as Sorin's breathing grew harsh. He struggled in Kaidyn's grip, crying out something in panic that Kaidyn could not make out.

"Sorin! It's only me, it's Kai, what's wrong?"

"Kai? Oh gods, I saw it. I *saw* it. Please don't make me watch again. I don't want to see—" Sorin covered his eyes, babbling, and Kaidyn fought to calm him.

"It was only a dream. There's nobody else here, nothing's going to harm you—"

"No, *no!* You don't understand. You can't stop it. Nobody can stop it! It's inside of me, and when I sleep it will come back. *Please* don't let me sleep, Kai—" Sorin was openly weeping now, pleading with him. He continued to shudder in his grasp long after Kaidyn had managed to quiet him.

" . . . It's all right now, I'm here. I'm not going anywhere. I swear I won't let you go . . ." Kaidyn kept up the litany of words, not really paying attention to what he said but understanding that his voice was more important than anything else, listening in mounting distress to Sorin's muffled sobs. He had never thought to see the usually self-possessed Sorin so fragile, so broken.

"You have to promise me Kai. You have to—I can't watch this anymore. I *can't*, but it won't go away. No matter what I do, even when I'm awake sometimes, I can see it happening like it's right in front of me. Promise me you won't leave. *Swear* it."

"I swear it," Kaidyn said, his voice as firm as he could make it and continuing to run his fingers across Sorin's shoulders and down his back. All the while, Kaidyn's mind raced at the implications of what Sorin was telling him.

Sorin had not said much, and it was plausible that he had simply become dizzy from exhaustion, stumbling and hitting his head with enough force to cause a faint. Something told Kaidyn, though, this was not the case.

Sorin had *seen* something—and snippets of conversation he had taken part in and overheard replayed in Kaidyn's mind. *"Sometimes my mind plays tricks on me, and I speak without really knowing what I say . . . I never asked for this, never wanted it . . ."*

He recalled the first time he'd awakened in this very bed and the way Sorin had seemed to be in pain. Sorin had almost needed assistance to rise from where he had been kneeling beside it. At the time, Kaidyn had tried to dismiss this as happenstance, not any business of his own. But when paired with the way Sorin's eyes had appeared to glaze over just a few minutes later, his face wiped unnervingly clean of all emotion, so unlike his usual demeanor . . .

Sorin shifted slightly, and Kaidyn spoke softly against his hair. "Sorin. Are you all right?"

Sorin seemed to come back to himself at the question and eased up. "My head hurts," he whispered, raising a hand to touch it gingerly. Then he looked at Kaidyn, eyes wide as he opened his mouth to pant. "Kai, I think I'm going to—"

Kaidyn grasped him by the shoulders, only just managing to save Sorin from falling to the floor as he bent over, head down and eyes streaming, to throw up the contents of his stomach.

Luckily for them both, Nora was no fool.

At some point after Kaidyn had finished cleaning up and putting the only half-conscious Sorin back to bed, there came a firm knock at the door. Kaidyn sat up, disentangling himself from his lover's arms without waking him, and went to let Nora into the house.

She did not bother with any pleasantries. "When you did not return, I thought I had best check on you myself." Outside, the wind had whipped up into a gale, and her dark healer's braid streamed out alongside her cloak.

"You mean check on Sorin," Kaidyn said, and Nora did not correct him.

"Is he sleeping?"

"Yes. But you'd best come in. I found him unconscious on the floor, and when he woke—"

Nora pushed past him, leaving Kaidyn to close the door and trail her to the bedchamber.

"How long has he been asleep?"

"An hour, perhaps. I think it's just exhaustion now, but . . ." Kaidyn left his sentence unfinished as Nora checked Sorin over, her expression giving nothing away. Sorin did not stir even when Nora pried his eyes open for a moment to examine them, and Kaidyn felt another stab of worry.

"Tell me what happened."

"Will Sorin be all right?"

"Yes. You're right. He's only sleeping now. He simply used up too much energy, and now — well, it is as you see. This is exactly what happens when people push their Gift too hard. I specifically warned him of this!"

"But that's not the whole of it." Kaidyn's voice was flat.

Nora sighed, allowing some of her own tiredness to show. "No, it's not. But tell me what happened here first, exactly as you remember it. Leave nothing out."

She listened in silence to Kaidyn's explanation. It did not take long, and for a few tense moments afterward, the only noise came from the wind battering at the shutters. Then Nora nodded decisively and gestured for him to follow her into the adjoining room, where they lit more candles and sat with their chairs angled so that they could still keep an eye on Sorin. Kaidyn did not expect him to wake any time soon, but could not bring himself to turn away.

He waited until Nora eventually broke the stillness. "You have questions, I'm sure. I will tell you what I can."

Kaidyn was under no illusions as to what she meant. "You once said it wasn't your secret to tell," he reminded her.

She looked at him, blue eyes dark and weary. "The time for secrets has passed. If you are to stay by his side — "

"I refuse to leave it," Kaidyn interrupted her, his voice coming out more sharply than he intended, and Nora almost smiled.

"Sorin was right. You *are* impatient — and proud, and fierce, and determined. Like a wolf, or perhaps one of the dragons of old." Kaidyn opened his mouth to speak again, but Nora waved him off. "No, don't say anything. I don't mean to point these things out as flaws. This time. But the fact remains, you must be made aware of certain things. It appears Sorin has told you nothing, which makes him about as stubborn as you are. But time is running out."

Kaidyn felt his heart speed up in apprehension at these last words. "Running out for what?"

Nora shook her head. "I do not know. Not for certain, at least, though I have my suspicions. Perhaps Sorin does not fully know either. Even if he did, he likely would not tell."

Kaidyn saw no point in not being direct. "He sees things, doesn't he? Bad things. Things that will happen, or might happen."

Nora frowned a little. "I doubt it's quite so straightforward as that. But to put it in plainest terms, yes."

"Visions. Or dreams. Or both."

"Yes."

"He has no control over them? When they happen, or what he sees in them?"

"None." Nora passed a hand over her face, and Kaidyn was reminded that Sorin was not simply another patient but also her cousin and her friend. "I thought at first it might be something he could learn to . . . contain, somewhat," she continued slowly. "To shape, or at the very least to limit his visions so that they did not take him so unawares. I'm beginning to think I was wrong."

"But there are warning signs," Kaidyn protested. "Ways to tell when they're coming."

"Would that it were so simple. He often gets headaches, as you've doubtless noticed, but he has since early childhood and not all seem to be connected. Exhaustion may increase the chances of him seeing something, but once again, that hasn't always proven to be the case."

"But if he was born with this ability then surely —"

"You don't understand, Kai!" She glared at him, and Kaidyn was a little shocked by her outburst. Nora never raised her voice, and in all the time he had known her he had never once seen such a break in composure, nor heard real fear behind her words. It was there now in the slight tremor of her voice, the way her hands were clenched tight in her lap.

She blinked hard, then carried on before Kaidyn could apologize or say anything more. "You don't know what it's like! Nobody does. Do you claim to understand the toll this has on him? Every time his head so much as aches or his body feels heavy, Sorin wonders if he'll see something that horrifies him. No, shut up, and just listen," she ordered when Kaidyn made to speak again.

"Sorin is afraid, and I'm not sure I even blame him for not telling you why. Is it better to tell someone when he sees a vision of them wounded and dying, to caution them and have them live in fear for the rest of their lives? Or should he meddle with fate and inadvertently be the very cause of the accident he seeks to prevent?" She shook her head in frustration. "And what of the people who have nothing at all to do with him? What is Sorin to do when he crosses paths with someone on the street he's never met in his life, only to realize he's dreamed of them? Pass them by and have the guilt at not having warned them consume him, or risk being carted away as a madman? There can be no right answer!" She paused, breathing a little heavily after this tirade, visibly seeking to regain her control.

Kaidyn averted his eyes, staring over instead at Sorin's unmoving shape. He thought about what it must be like going through every single day in fear of witnessing something awful and being completely unable to speak of it. What horrors had Sorin seen over the years—seen, and kept entirely to himself?

" . . . I had no idea," Kaidyn admitted in a low voice.

Nora's expression softened. "No. And you still don't. Neither do I. Only Sorin can ever truly know."

A thought struck Kaidyn then and he started, feeling sick to his stomach. "If this . . . this so-called Gift is inherent, does that mean he's been seeing these things from when he was too young to even comprehend—"

Nora looked grimmer than Kaidyn had ever seen her. "Do you know what he told me once?"

Kaidyn wasn't sure he wanted to know the answer. Mutely, he shook his head.

"He said that one day, his mother happened upon him with a needle in his hand. He had planned to blind himself, convinced that if he could not see then he would no longer have to witness the visions either." She paused. "It was his sixth name day."

There could be no reply to this. There was nothing Kaidyn could say that was capable of fully expressing his shock or his sudden, furious anger for whatever it was that forced Sorin to look on, helpless, as he saw time and time again things that nobody should ever have to watch. And as for Kaidyn himself—he was as helpless to defend Sorin as Sorin was of shielding himself.

There seemed nothing more to say after that. Kaidyn and Nora sat for several long minutes, each thinking their own thoughts and listening to the wind howl. Sorin was a motionless form in the bed as he slept on, blessedly at peace. *But for how long?*

Eventually, Nora roused herself and stood, glancing over at Kaidyn. "I must go back," she said, her voice returned to its usual measured tone. "There's nothing more I can do here, and there are still others who need my help. I'll be sleeping in the infirmary again tonight, should he have need of me."

"I'm staying here."

"Good. I will make it clear to the head instructor that I've given you permission to do so."

"His permission matters little to me. I would stay regardless." He half-thought Nora might respond to this, perhaps scold him for speaking so disrespectfully of his superiors to her face, but she only nodded as if she expected nothing less.

Kaidyn accompanied her to the door. She stopped at the threshold and turned back to face him, her gaze clear and steady. "I'll be back first thing in the morning. Kai . . ."

"Yes?"

"You might not be able to protect him from this, but you *are* a comfort to him. I am his friend and have known his family for many years, but you . . . you're something else to him entirely. Sorin trusts you. As do I."

"I know." The knowledge brought him no particular joy this night, but his hands clenched involuntarily, as if he was determined to physically fend off whatever threatened to cause Sorin harm.

Nora lifted her brows. "You're in love with him."

She was not the first to make that statement. But Kaidyn knew it himself now and saw no point in denying it. Nora smiled, surprising him. "You might think it odd, but I'm glad of it. You're what he needs." The wind could not quite drown out her parting words. "And whether you accept it or not, he is what you need as well."

CHAPTER EIGHT

Several days later, the snows began.

Though Sorin had seemingly made a full recovery following his collapse, Kaidyn kept close watch on him and was aware of Nora doing the same. Sorin ignored them both and went about his business as though nothing had changed. Taking his cue, Kaidyn made no mention of what had passed, still unsure of what he could do to help beyond simply being there should Sorin have need of him.

Still, not everything could fall back into place so easily. For all his even temperament and easygoing nature, Sorin did not smile as much as he used to, and Kaidyn could tell he only allowed himself to completely relax when they were alone together. All too aware of his own limitations, Kaidyn attempted to distract Sorin at every opportunity in the weeks that followed.

They bundled themselves up in heavy layers and attended the annual snow festival, forming teams and pelting snowballs at each other along with hundreds of other townspeople until they were red-faced and breathless with laughter. They ate steaming bowls of the town's special winter soup, Kaidyn grinning in amusement as Sorin's eyes watered from the large amounts of spice.

They hired horses and rode out to a lonely place near the mountains, where Kaidyn watched Sorin's face transform in wonder at the perfectly frozen waterfall, brighter than cut diamond. They walked up a hill when it was time for the palace to hold their midwinter lantern display, spreading out blankets far above the rest of the crowds and lying on their stomachs to stare down at the night view. They spent countless hours simply being near one another—talking and sleeping and loving—until it seemed they were the only two people in existence, and the rest of the world only a dream.

But none of this could make the tightly coiled anxiety disappear entirely, and Kaidyn was aware they both knew it. It played constantly on Kaidyn's mind, distracting him during training and making his expression pensive enough that Sorin finally brought it up himself one afternoon, as they walked to his townhouse from the academy.

"You've been very quiet lately," he said.

"Have I?"

"Yes. Tell me what you're thinking about?"

Kaidyn opened his mouth, wondering what to say. As much as Kaidyn sometimes felt it would be better to discuss it, he could not face the fear and pain that would inevitably cloud Sorin's expression at the mere mention of it.

But Sorin was looking up at him expectantly, snowflakes gathering in his hair, and Kaidyn said the first thing that came to his mind. "Will you go to the masquerade ball with me?"

Sorin's expression in that instant was priceless. "I—what?"

"I said, will you go to the ball with me?"

"Your mother's ball?"

"Yes."

"The one the palace holds every year to celebrate the close of winter?"

"Yes."

Sorin's tone changed slightly. "The one you once told me you always hated having to attend?"

"The very same."

"Kai, I . . . if you're only asking me out of—"

"Sorin." Kaidyn looked directly at him, clasping both of Sorin's hands in his own and keeping them there. "I *want* to go. With you." And he realized that he did, very much. "It's true, I did hate it, ever since I was too old to cling to my mother's skirts and saw what people really thought of my kind. But I must go regardless, and I thought . . . with you by my side, I might . . ."

Sorin appeared a little apprehensive, but there was also a glow about him as he nodded, suddenly breathless. "All right." He looked down. "I've never been to the palace before. I confess, I'm nervous at the thought."

"I am too," Kaidyn admitted. "I have not paid visit to court there in months. Were it not for my mother . . ." A thought struck him then. "But surely you must have been to many grand balls before—I would have thought your name guaranteed it."

"Ah." Sorin looked a little embarrassed now. "As few as I could that my family did not host themselves. I have never been fond of large gatherings, or the attention that came with it. As I grew older it got to the point where I rarely left the estate. Had it not been for Nora's letter urging me to join her here, I would likely still be living with my parents in the countryside." He bit his lip in a familiar gesture. "I'm afraid I have little idea of what to expect. Or what to wear, come to think of it. Gods, people talk of your mother's masquerade as though it's some kind of fantasy."

Kaidyn grinned, remembering some of what he'd seen and wondering how Sorin might react to it. The masquerade was certainly unlike any other ball he'd ever witnessed. Though it by no means marked the end of the cold, it was the first sign for most of the coming spring, and people celebrated in kind. Masks and elaborate costumes did not describe even half of it. The ball had indeed evolved over the years into a kind of fantastical escape for people seeking a release from pent-up energies and the frustrations of winter.

Some women dressed as men, and some men as women. Others played at being servants or household retainers in order to leave the rules of society behind for the space of a single night. Unlike most formal balls, names were not publicly announced upon entrance, and anyone with an invitation could attend. Most took the opportunity to forget or reinvent themselves in some fashion — aided, of course, by an endlessly flowing amount of wine.

Wild rumors of what took place at these balls were talked about for weeks afterward, and Kaidyn could well imagine that such an event might seem intimidating to someone with little experience in such things. He tilted Sorin's face up so that he could briefly quell his fears the best way he knew how. "I would not complain should you choose to wear a burlap sack, so long as I might be the one to escort you in it."

Sorin gave a shaky laugh at the image. "I imagine I can do a little better."

"I imagine you can. But in fact, I don't care about any of that. Not one bit."

"No?"

"No."

And not wanting to waste the chance, Kaidyn kissed him again — unmindful of the snow that continued to tumble noiselessly around them, nor that they stood in the middle of the road where anyone might bear witness. He didn't mind anything else in the world in that moment, so long as they had this.

"You're early."

Nora stepped out of Sorin's house, closing the door behind her, and Kaidyn blinked. Though not unwelcome, he had not expected to see her this evening. "I didn't know how bad the roads would be — I thought the carriage might be slow going with the crowds," he replied. "Where's Sorin?"

Nora looked like she was fighting back laughter. "He'll be out in a moment."

Right on cue the door opened again, and a person who was most definitely not his lover stepped out. Unless, of course, Sorin happened to be wearing a deep sapphire-colored gown with sweeping skirts and delicately puffed sleeves, complete with upswept hair and lacy, wrist-length gloves in matching black.

Kaidyn gaped. "*Sorin?*"

Sorin's fingers twined together. One of them held a plain dark mask. "Um. Yes."

"Why — what — how did you — "

"Nora helped." Sorin stared at the ground. "If the masquerade is an escape, then I wanted to be able to do it properly." He paused, obviously anxious. " . . . Are you angry with me?"

Kaidyn managed to get hold of himself and stepped closer. It was certainly astonishing — never in his wildest dreams had he imagined Sorin in a dress. The subtle patterning on the bodice leading up to a high collar even created the illusion of a slight curve. Still, once he got over the initial shock of it . . .

Kaidyn reached out to tug gently at one of the escaping strands of hair. "I'm not angry," he said, and let the beginnings of his grin show. "I don't know if it would be a compliment or not by saying that you make a fairly convincing woman, though." This was at least partly true, though there was nothing especially feminine about Sorin's face. No doubt the mask was intended to help disguise that.

Sorin smiled back, relieved. "I know this probably wasn't what you had in mind when you asked if I might be your escort."

"He should be grateful to be allowed to escort you at all, a pretty thing like you," Nora chimed in, her expression reflecting her amusement. "And I admit, I am relieved that gown may finally see some use. It was a gift, thoughtfully given, albeit not quite to my taste." She shuddered in mock-disgust, and Kaidyn grinned, trying to imagine her in such a gown and failing. He had rarely seen her in anything other than dark, practical clothing, usually loose-fitting and unadorned by lace or other finery.

He turned his attention back to Sorin and swept into a bow. "Well then." Taking hold of Sorin's hand, he brought it to his lips in one fluid motion born from many years of enforced practice. "It is an honor, my lady. And who do I have the pleasure of escorting this evening?"

Sorin's lips parted in a round *oh* of realization. "I hadn't even thought of a name," he said, looking a little panicked.

Kaidyn could not pass the opportunity by. "How about Bertha?" he suggested.

Sorin huffed a laugh and went along with it, hands on his hips in a pretense of offended indignation. "Do I look like a Bertha to you?"

"Perhaps not. How foolish of me. Well then, what of Juris? Especially when you make that face. No? Stop me when I hit upon one you like. Hateen. Mayvis. Doloren. Ag—"

"Enough. Simply take the feminine version of his name and be done with it," Nora interrupted them, stamping her feet in the cold.

Kaidyn turned to look at her. "Sora?"

Nora shrugged. "Why not? Better to pick something close to Sorin if you have any chance of fooling anyone, since he's an awful liar. I even have another relative named Sora, so if somebody asks if my cousin attended the ball I can quite honestly say yes. Now stop dithering, you two. It's freezing, and I don't wish to keep standing out here in the snow."

Kaidyn nodded. "Sora it is then," he said. And then, more

seriously, "You are beautiful, Sora. Sorin."

"So are you," Sorin replied, and Kaidyn knew an unaccustomed moment of self-consciousness. He had decided to forgo a mask this evening. His height and hair usually made him instantly recognizable anyway, and with Sorin on his arm he had resolved to go as himself or not at all. For once, Kaidyn felt oddly proud of this. He too had made an effort with his appearance—his clothes were new, his boots polished to a high shine. He had allowed his hair to grow over the past weeks, and though still too short to be bound in the proper manner befitting a nobleman, he had brushed it until it lay thick and glossy.

As though reading his mind, Sorin smiled and reached out to brush a hand over his cheek in the same instant that Kaidyn found himself leaning forward. They both paused, bodies not quite touching, each waiting for the other to make a move. The moment stretched out between them—a heartbeat caught in time.

Nora cleared her throat.

Sorin jumped, the spell abruptly broken. "Time enough for such things later, I'm sure," Nora said, although there was no real annoyance in her tone.

At least she had given Kaidyn the chance to remember how to breathe. "Indeed." He took Sorin by the hand again. "We will take our leave then. If I may?" He turned to Sorin again, ready to hand him into the carriage.

"Thank you, Nora," Sorin said somewhat belatedly, finding his voice again as Kaidyn helped him inside.

Nora waved them off, looking suspiciously amused at her cousin's sudden bashfulness.

They made good time, though Sorin seemed unsure of exactly where to look as the carriage trundled down crowded streets. Other carriages soon fell into line behind them. The taverns were noisy tonight with their own celebrations despite the cold, the presence of the City Watch more conspicuous than usual. There had been no work that day, and many revelers had begun drinking long before dark. Thankfully, the ground was still frozen hard, not yet turned to mud and slush, and the carriages proceeded without incident through the town.

They passed rows upon rows of guards and attendants, who checked invitations as the pair made their way up the road leading to the palace. The path was lit by lines of burning torches. By the time the horses slowed and eventually stopped altogether, Kaidyn could hear the strands of music coming from the dance hall and people spilling from lines leading to the entrance. He smelled the veritable waves of perfume on the air.

"I'm even more nervous than I thought I would be," Sorin confessed as they exited the safety of the carriage.

"Don't be. If anyone should be nervous, it's me. This is supposed to be my home, and yet . . ." Their hands met, fingers weaving together in mutual reassurance.

"Then I suppose we are well matched," Sorin laughed, clearly making an effort to shake off his unease.

"My lord? My lady? May I assist you into the ballroom?" Kaidyn shook his head, dismissing the hovering servants. Keeping hold of Sorin's hand, he walked inside with his head lifted, ready to meet the gaze of anyone who chose to whisper or stare. He was Kaidyn Riverveil, and tonight of all nights, with Sorin by his side, he was not ashamed of it.

"Mother. It is good to see you again." Kaidyn stooped to kiss the queen's heavily powdered cheek, and she pulled her son closer without hesitation, uncaring that many others stood waiting to greet her.

"My son." He thought her voice trembled slightly, though it was difficult to tell amid the noise of the ballroom. "How

I've missed you."

Kaidyn knew he owed his mother an apology. Going out of his way to avoid becoming entangled in the social politics of court also meant cutting himself off even from those who genuinely cared for him. He was aware that despite her welcoming smile, she still felt the wound his absence had caused.

"I am sorry, mother. Truly. But it really is good to see you," he told her, meaning it.

He was rewarded with a smile that was, if not as joyous as he remembered, then at least honest. "Kaidyn," she spoke his name fondly. "You look very handsome this evening. And I see you've grown your hair again. It quite suits you, my dear."

"You look wonderful too, mother."

This was a half-truth. The queen did indeed look beautiful, resplendent in a trailing gown of white and gold with voluminous sleeves that reached almost to the ground. Her hair, too, had been left loose to tumble almost to the floor instead of being pinned out of the way as usual, making her appear young and girlish. But Kaidyn had not overlooked the thick layer of make-up, and guessed it was there to hide not wrinkles but instead the tell-tale signs of fatigue. She was also far thinner than the last time he had seen her.

Though she did not even come to the height of his shoulder, the queen had never been a frail woman. He had always known her to be full-figured and full of life, with round cheeks and laughing eyes. Now even her hair appeared faded, her entire being in some way drained.

Kaidyn knew his mother usually enjoyed the sparkle and glamour of balls, the costumes and the dancing, but he also knew her position was more burden to her than joy. She was a queen, yet she preferred flowers to jewels, used to smell always of spring, had run and danced and sang despite the responsibilities that weighed upon her.

Was it my father who gave her at least the illusion of a more carefree existence? How hard has it been for her to maintain that pretense after she sent him away? Kaidyn wondered if she yearned for freedom—in much the same way he himself did—now that her two children were grown and she had no other immediate relatives to support her. Perhaps she secretly yearned to have his father back, despite seeming as though she no longer grieved the loss of their love. He tried to let none of these thoughts show as he was released from his mother's embrace. Her eyes widened slightly as she took in Sorin standing closely behind him.

"And who is your most charming escort this evening?"

Kaidyn stepped back to take Sorin's arm. "Mother, may I introduce the Lady Sora, who arrived in the capital this past summer. My lady, I am pleased for you to meet my mother and sovereign, Queen Fianah Riverveil."

"But you must simply call me Fianah," his mother added with a dimpled smile, quickly dispensing with the formalities. "For anyone Kaidyn wishes to accompany him is welcome in my home."

"Your Majesty." Sorin dipped into what was, Kaidyn thought, a passable curtsy, given his lack of practice, and smiled back at the queen. "We became familiar through the Lady Nora, who I believe you are also acquainted with. It is my pleasure to be Kai's escort tonight. And you are quite right—he *is* very handsome."

A look of surprised flitted briefly over the queen's face before she grasped Sorin spontaneously by the hands. "You are a treasure, my dear. You see, Kaidyn? Everyone can see what a fine man you've become."

"Yes, mother," Kaidyn dutifully agreed. Then, once she had released an unexpectedly blushing Sorin, he moved closer again and lowered his voice. "Mother. How are you really?" he asked.

For the space of a breath, Kaidyn could plainly see it — the pain and the helplessness that imprisoned her.

Then the queen laughed and the expression was wiped clean, hidden away under a show of bright chatter. "My, such seriousness! I am perfectly well, my Kai." Clearly, Sorin's casual use of Kaidyn's name had not gone unmarked. "I do hope the . . . Lady Sora enjoys herself tonight. Take good care of him, my dear." She directed this last at Sorin. "He is a stubborn child, but his heart is true."

"I know it well," Sorin replied, and the queen was all smiles again as she bid them both a good evening, begging Kaidyn to come and visit her again at the palace soon before turning to greet her next guests.

Sorin heaved a sigh as they walked away from her, arm in arm. "Your mother is an interesting woman," he said to Kaidyn in an undertone. "And certainly no fool."

"No, though I believe she sometimes hides exactly how much she knows. It was so when I was a child, too." Those days seemed impossibly far away now.

"She certainly knows about me," Sorin said wryly.

"It would not surprise me. But rest assured my mother is not in the habit of spilling secrets. Your identity is safe with her."

"Oh. Well, yes, but I daresay she knew about me long before tonight."

Kaidyn stopped walking, a little puzzled. "What do you mean?"

"Why, I should think Nora would have told her long ago."

"But why? They know each other, of course. Nora used to be Court Healer and still comes to call at the palace sometimes. She is said to be one of the best healers in the kingdom, after all. But I don't believe she and my mother are particularly close."

"Kai... of course they're close. They've been good friends for years, and I assume a great deal more than that."

"What?" Kaidyn frowned, still nonplussed. "I'm sure Nora would have told me if..." He paused, eyebrows raised at what Sorin was implying. "Are you sure?"

"Would it bother you if I was?"

"I..." The idea was certainly a foreign one. Kaidyn had not thought his mother had taken another lover after his father had left, and it was even stranger to imagine her with the brisk, business-like Nora. He could scarce imagine two women less alike, either in appearance or manner. *Can they really be so much closer than I had imagined?*

"I don't think it bothers me," Kaidyn finally replied. "I just... never pictured it, especially since it was Nora who chose to leave the palace and work at the academy in the first place. She's been there for years now. Besides, Nora would never—" He stopped as a thought struck him.

"Would never want to mix her professional and private life?" Sorin finished for him.

"I suppose it's not the kind of thing you would tell a young child," Kaidyn mused.

"Especially not your own child, I would guess!" Sorin grinned and his hand tightened around Kaidyn's. "I am happy for Nora. Happy for them both. The queen must have been very lonely after your father left."

"Yes, I think she was, though she never complained of it. If you are right, then I'm happy for them too—but I think perhaps I won't tell Nora that." His shiver of fear was only half in jest.

Sorin laughed. "Then let us put it from our minds for now. Dance with me."

"With pleasure." Kaidyn swept Sorin onto the floor, joining the myriad of other couples in carefully-pressed trousers and shirts, jewel-bright gowns in rich silks and brocaded velvets, and fantastic masks and wigs. He was surprised to realize he was enjoying himself.

Sorin was practically glowing, taking in the array of colorful and elaborate masks on display and exclaiming in delight at the fancy dress of the guests. Some, like Sorin, were clearly in some form of disguise or charade, while others were dressed as animals or storybook creatures, having hired artisans to paint their faces. Large headdresses, glittering precious stones, and many other bold and arresting displays met their eyes wherever they looked.

The room was filled with the noise and laughter of hundreds of people — all of whom were there to show off and be anyone but themselves for the evening. Kaidyn once thought he saw Emil somewhere among the revelers, mask pushed up and head thrown back in laughter at some joke or comment, but he quickly lost sight of the man and could not be sure.

Flushed and happy with wine, Sorin chatted shamelessly with other courtiers, accepting offers to dance from some but always returning to Kaidyn. They shared goblets of wine back and forth, not minding the intimacy this implied. Kaidyn had fun pointing out anyone he thought Sorin might find interesting or amusing.

"The woman in the butter-yellow dress and improbably high shoes is the Lady Sulandra Myles, who drank so much last year that she passed out on the staircase." Then he pointed to a man with a tiny beard, dressed as a hunstman. "That gentleman is Lord Braxton Humboldt. He spent his father's entire fortune gambling on horses, then won it all back in a single evening in a stunning game of cards."

Sorin flicked his gaze to the elderly woman wearing a tiara so studded with gems that it was difficult to look at, Kaidyn following it. "That's the Countess Elleanor Trost. Rumor has it that her late husband was a terrible businessman, and that she more than tripled the family's wealth after she took over the household."

Sorin laughed and pointed out various other figures, en- joying the descriptions Kaidyn gave. "What of the lady in green whose skirts are so big she could barely fit through the door? . . . The portly gentleman in the red sash and feathered mask? . . . The tiny woman with the towering wig? . . ."

Kaidyn himself was easily identifiable with neither mask nor costume and escorting an unknown aristocrat on his arm. But despite plenty of stares in his direction, he made it through most of the evening feeling remarkably calm. Used to gritting his teeth at the raised eyebrows and thinly-veiled contempt dealt to him from preening nobles, he found it an altogether new experience. Though the gentry's petty arro- gance and narrow-minded disdain still rankled, he was able to put it aside this night. Instead, he focused on the light in Sorin's eyes and the way he felt in his arms as they danced.

"Oh! I'm so sorry, my lady." The woman Sorin had bumped into was dressed in a gown of brilliant turquoise, her dark hair piled elegantly atop her head.

"Not at all, it was my—" She froze in the act of waving off Sorin's apology, her gaze now fixed instead on Kaidyn.

Kaidyn stared back.

"Brother. It has been a long time." She removed her mask.

"Lyrah. I . . . yes. It has." Kaidyn tried to remember the last time they had even met face to face, but he could not.

Recovered from her surprise, his sister seemed as coolly poised as ever. She was small and neat-featured, no taller than her mother and not prone to gaudiness, but it had been many years since Kaidyn had been comfortable in her pres- ence. Her every measured glance felt like a judgment.

"Have you been well?"

"Yes, I thank you. Have you?" He was a child again, re- duced to banalities in front of his sister's effortless composure.

She inclined her head. "Indeed. It is good of you to ask. And your companion?"

"Of course. Forgive my belated introductions."

Kaidyn went through the motions of acquainting them, feeling stiff and awkward, knowing that Sorin must sense his tension. They exchanged a few more strained pleasantries before his sister, with a murmured apology toward Sorin, directed her words to Kaidyn alone.

"I expect you will be glad to see the end of winter, brother."

"Oh?" He tried to mimic her composure, but her very presence after so many years spent purposefully avoiding his company was disconcerting.

"You never used to cease talking of service to your nation. Of proving yourself to be as brave as your namesake. Do you not remember? But perhaps you have put such dreams of your childhood behind you."

"Sister?" He could not make sense of her words.

"The Council has not been spending the long cold idly. I had simply wondered what your own plans were, when the snows melt and your time at the academy comes to an end."

Perhaps she, too, was avoiding having to address him by name. "I don't know. I suppose I will be assigned a position to aid in the war as best I may."

"I am glad to hear you say it. There are those in the kingdom who seem rather less disposed to defend it."

He could not understand her sudden interest in him, nor completely follow the conversation. *Is she referring to other Half-Bloods?*

"We who are charged with doing so must not hesitate to use any means necessary," she continued when Kaidyn did not respond. "And once the snows melt, allowing our armies to move freely again, we will of course allow you to play your part in it. As everyone in our fair kingdom must."

Kaidyn was suddenly cold. "I don't—"

"Forgive my rudeness. Such matters are perhaps not appropriate to discuss in the midst of a ball." Lyrah studied his face for a moment. "I should not have spoken thus." She seemed genuinely regretful. "Please, go back to the celebrations, and rest assured that I will fulfill my duties. I will guide the Council to act in the best interests of the kingdom if I must. Mother will not need to put her own health in jeopardy."

Though the words were spoken politely, Kaidyn was unable to suppress his reaction. He took a step back, grabbing Sorin by the hand as he did so, and there was an uncomfortable silence before Lyrah gathered her skirts and nodded a farewell.

"Brother. Lady Sora. I pray you enjoy the rest of the evening. If you will excuse me." Lyrah's parting left them standing motionless in her wake. Kaidyn watched her walk purposefully in the direction of the queen, still surrounded by a flock of courtiers. He watched as his mother's smile faltered and her body seemingly shrank even smaller as Lyrah approached her.

" . . . Kai?" Sorin asked, and Kaidyn wondered what emotions were playing over his face for his lover to sound so hesitant.

"Yes?" His voice was distant even to his own ears.

The weight of Sorin's hand on his arm was a reassurance. "You're trembling. Are you all right?"

He was indeed trembling, although Kaidyn did not know if it was out of shock or fear. "Yes." Sorin merely looked at him. "No."

"Would you like to leave?"

It was as uncomplicated as that. Sorin saw right through Kaidyn, just as he had done from the very beginning.

"Yes. Yes, please."

Kaidyn did not talk of returning to the academy on their

way back, and Sorin did not suggest it. They returned to Sorin's townhouse together and did not speak, only hurried each other inside, where they tore off one another's garments with a kind of urgency that had never before been present in their lovemaking.

Their mouths met hard and swift as Kaidyn removed the pins binding Sorin's hair. His lover pulled him closer, gasping his name. They tumbled onto the bed in a frenzy, Sorin on his back and Kaidyn atop him, pinning him by the wrists and grinding down, making Sorin cry out again.

"Please, oh gods please, Kai—"

Kaidyn ran his hands feverishly over Sorin's lean form, through the dark spill of his hair, and leaned down to capture his mouth in another bruising kiss. Sorin surged up frantically to meet him. They tangled together in a tempest of limbs, panting and burning.

At some point Kaidyn tried to pull away, worried he was hurting Sorin, but Sorin only shook his head and dragged Kaidyn back down, betraying his own need.

Their union was sharp and breathtaking, painful and bittersweet, and long past the point of gentleness or restraint.

They could both feel it. The end was approaching as surely as the dawn.

CHAPTER NINE

Spring arrived in a flurry of petals, palest lavender, and creamy white—the colors of change.

It should have been beautiful, but the growing warmth and gradual lengthening of the days did nothing to assuage the tension that held Kaidyn tight in its grip, and he was aware that Sorin felt it just as keenly. Kaidyn knew his lover was not sleeping well at night—the dark circles, almost bruise-like, beneath his eyes said it for him. He wondered if it was sleeplessness or if, like himself, Sorin, was plagued by barely-remembered yet disturbing dreams whose meanings he could not discern.

He had little time to dwell on this, however. Training at the academy intensified as instructors worked their students harder than ever, seeking to hone the skills of the men who would soon become fully-fledged officers. Kaidyn welcomed the distraction, throwing himself into his training with a vengeance.

There was precious little time now for Kaidyn and Sorin to be alone, and whenever they were able to snatch a few hours of privacy, both avoided speaking of what had occurred at the ball. It was as if they would be tempting fate by talking of it, bringing whatever premonition they had both felt closer to reality. Instead, they filled the silence with other things, harmless things that blunted the edges of their fears—for a time at least.

The time eventually came for Kaidyn to make good on his word to his mother and visit the palace once more. By unspoken agreement, Sorin accompanied him on the journey there. However, he insisted he would walk the grounds while Kaidyn went on inside. "You and your mother should be able to speak alone," he said.

When Kaidyn protested, insisting that she would be delighted to meet him again, Sorin only smiled and said a little sadly, "It is not yet time." He did not explain further, and Kaidyn knew enough not to press him.

They braved the still chilly winds and went to the palace on foot from the academy. The walk took up much of the morning and had warmed them by the time they arrived. The palace looked entirely different by daylight. It was peaceful, but too quiet, even desolate. Their progress was unhurried and largely ignored by the few people going about their business, for which Kaidyn would have normally been grateful. Now the lack of noise made the atmosphere seem somber and lifeless.

The main courtyard in particular, which had once been bustling with courtiers no matter the hour, appeared all but abandoned. Many of the trees were bare of leaves even though it was past the time when they should have been flowering. Their limbs stood brown and skeletal, rattling against one another in the wind. Other spots stood entirely empty, only cold earth in place of bushes and plants that had been uprooted and not replaced.

Not wanting to add to the cheerlessness, Kaidyn pointed out to Sorin things that caught his eye. "This was a statue that had been built long ago by an ancestor famous for his Gift of stone-working . . . That building comprises the guest quarters, where I often sought solitude as a child . . . Over there is the entrance to the orchard, where the fruit used to spill from the trees in amounts so large that I and the other children from the palace made ourselves sick trying to eat it all."

"It seems . . . somewhat emptier than I expected," Sorin admitted, as they sat on the terrace steps to view the courtyard from above. "And not only because we are nearly the only people here."

"It used to be a far more vibrant place," Kaidyn acknowledged. "There were gardens once. In the height of summer, it was like walking through a maze, one so bright and so colorful it was difficult to know where to look."

"No longer? It is too cold yet for certain plants to bloom, I know, but the spaces on either side of the pathways are completely bare."

"Mother used to take care of the gardens." Kaidyn stared down at his hands. "She loves pretty things, and they were her pride and joy. The flowers blossomed from her Gift, largely untended by the palace gardeners. Some even say that flowers sprang into being wherever she trod barefoot upon the earth, though I don't know if such stories are true."

"An impressive Gift nonetheless," Sorin marveled.

"Yet it is whispered that she has not used her Gift in some time. I do not know if she . . ." It seemed almost traitorous to suggest that the queen was unable to summon her Gift. In many old tales, this was said be divine punishment for some misdeed or other, or a portent of worse things to come. Sorin gave Kaidyn a searching look but did not enquire further.

"A shame the flowers no longer bloom," he merely commented. "I imagine this would be a glorious sight otherwise."

"It was. It was the same in the northern palace as well, though I've not been there since I was a boy. I suppose the courtyard there looks much as this one does now, or worse. It has been long abandoned, and even with enough rain, the flowers would have quickly died without mother's Gift to sustain them."

"You miss it." Sorin was as quick to read behind the

words as always, even when Kaidyn hadn't realized what he was thinking until he spoke them.

He could do nothing but be honest in return, no matter how it hurt to remember. "I miss having a home."

Sorin stood from where he had been crouching, moving to face Kaidyn fully and waiting until Kaidyn was forced to meet his eyes. It was as if Sorin could see right into him, gleaning all of Kaidyn's secrets and exposing every one of his weaknesses to the light — and against all odds, cherishing him anyway.

Another chill gust of wind shook the branches around them, but Sorin did not move. "You will see that courtyard again one day," he said quietly. "This I promise you." Then he blinked and stepped back, absentmindedly rubbing his head. "Now you had best go in. You should not keep your mother waiting. She will be happy to see you."

But for once, Sorin was wrong.

Kaidyn found the passage leading to his mother's chambers barred by a string of pinch-faced guards. The leader informed Kaidyn with an icy politeness that the queen was indisposed and wished to see nobody — not even her own son.

Kaidyn stood by stubbornly, trying not to let his anger or his apprehension show. "Will you not at least tell her I am here? If she is not feeling well, I will wait. All day if I must."

But neither his questions nor his stubbornness got him anywhere, and his repeated requests to notify his mother of his presence were ignored. The guard would say only that the queen herself had issued clear instructions. She was not to be disturbed under any circumstances. Not even the crown princess herself could have ordered them to allow Kaidyn passage.

Eventually, baffled and anxious, he was left with no choice but to leave without catching even a glimpse of the one person he had come to see. Neither had he seen his sister or a single member of the Council—a small blessing that did nothing to dispel his uneasiness, for he was, Kaidyn realized, far more powerless than even he had suspected.

In the following weeks he attempted to visit his mother several times more, only to be greeted with the same and ever more disconcerting outcome. The message was clear. The queen did not wish to see anyone. Kaidyn was not welcome. Although he had never been able to call more than a small handful of people friends, this latest change made Kaidyn even more aware of his isolation.

Even Nora, who had been a highly respected figure in the palace for many years, was not admitted into the queen's presence. She could only shake her head, troubled, when Kaidyn questioned her about it. If the queen was truly ill, then Nora should have received an official summons, yet she had heard nothing from the queen or her attendants, official or otherwise. If Sorin had been correct when he guessed that Nora and his mother were lovers, this news was all the more unsettling.

The season marched on, and he graduated from the academy alongside some two hundred fellow trainees.

Speeches were held, hands were shaken, and Kaidyn took in almost none of it. Sorin was an expressionless figure seated next to Nora on the podium outside, but Kaidyn felt both pairs of eyes on him as he took his turn to receive his congratulations. He kept his own expression equally blank, but could not help but feel bolstered by the fact that two people at least still thought well of him.

Kaidyn's circle was not as small as he had thought, though. As he stood apart from the other soldiers after the graduation ceremony, a clear space distancing him from most of the now relaxed and laughing soon-to-be officers, someone came up behind him to clap him on the back. Kaidyn tensed before turning to see who it was.

"Well done," Emil said, and there was nothing in his voice but an easy camaraderie, free of contempt or scorn. Kaidyn could only gape at him for a moment, and Emil looked as though he might laugh.

"It can't have been easy here, I know. But like I said that day, not everyone here is against you. And you didn't exactly help matters . . . but you *did* help me that day of the accident, despite your mistrust. So . . ." He extended his hand, and Kaidyn, still not able to fully process what was happening, automatically shook it.

Emil smiled. "Congratulations. And thank you. You're a good man, Kaidyn Riverveil, no matter what anyone else might think. I hope the day comes when more people will be able to see it."

It was perhaps only a small thing, but this encounter warmed Kaidyn the rest of the day. It lightened his step and caused him to question whether he had been too hasty to judge most full-blooded citizens of the kingdom, particularly those of noble birth. He knew the majority of them looked down on him and others of his kind. Their foul treatment of Half-Bloods was undeniable. *And yet how many others are eager, or at least open-minded enough, for change? How many times, in all my anger and bitterness, have I wrongly perceived to be against me? How many times have I mistaken silence for disdain, reserve for hatred?*

When the afternoon began to wane and he was able to leave the academy, Sorin noticed the difference in him immediately. "It's the first time I've seen you smile like that since the ball," he said, slipping his hand into Kaidyn's.

"Something happened after the ceremony today." He explained what had occurred with Emil and watched Sorin's face light up.

"That's one more person in the world who ignores old prejudices and can see someone for who they truly are."

"One man," Kaidyn reminded him gently, knowing how

passionate Sorin was about such matters.

But Sorin shook his head. "That is exactly how the world changes, Kai. A single person at a time, patterns of thinking slowly shifting until one day, you suddenly realize that what was once taken for granted is no longer the norm."

Kaidyn glanced at him. "I would once have told you that that idea was little better than fantasy."

"You see? So even the opinion of one as stubborn as you has changed in less than the course of a year," Sorin grinned before growing serious again. "This is the world I am hoping for, Kai. It is the world that *will* come to pass someday, if for no other reason than because those such as you and Emil are altering their perceptions of what is truth, and what is only an idea people have come to accept as truth."

They were silent a while then, walking close enough for their shoulders to brush, unconsciously treading a path toward the river until Sorin eventually spoke again. "What will you do now?" he asked.

Kaidyn could hear the low murmur of the water filtering its way through the trees. "I don't know. What else is there to do but wait?" *Wait to be told where to go. Wait to be assigned a position and sent off to war like so many others.* He did not say these things, but Sorin must have known he was thinking them.

"What is it you *want* to do?" Sorin amended.

Kaidyn thought about it, once again taken aback by the things that filled his own mind. "I want to help make a difference."

"Oh?" Sorin angled his head, looking up at him.

It was almost laughable, how easily the words now came from his mouth. Luck would certainly have laughed, Kaidyn thought, and he smiled wryly at himself. He had indeed changed if he had become so naive. He would never have called himself an idealist.

"I want to help build the place of which you speak. I don't even know whether I believe such a thing is possible, but the idea of helping to build a kingdom where I and others of like blood can live in peace . . . well. Perhaps today I caught my first glimpse of that."

Sorin was quiet again at this, but his expression was one Kaidyn hoped he would never forget.

They reached the river and stood for a while, just watching. Only a few weeks ago it had still been frozen over. Now it flowed freely again, the current strong as though making up for lost time. Sorin's voice, when it came, was soft but firm. "You can help create that place, Kai. I know it."

They sat, letting the sound of the bubbling water fill the clearing, and Sorin leaned against Kaidyn and closed his eyes. And though they remained like that for some time, they did not speak again, content to let the peace steal over them.

But their serenity was short-lived.

The palace soldiers waiting outside the gates of the academy were Kaidyn's first warning that something was amiss. The soldiers had been talking to one another in low voices, leaning against the pillars of the gate with their arms folded casually, but hastily snapped to attention as they spotted Kaidyn's approach. He heard Sorin draw in a sharp breath before one of them spoke.

"Kaidyn Riverveil," the soldier spoke formally. "You are to accompany us the palace at once."

"Why?" It was Sorin who asked, but the guards spared only a glance his way before continuing to address Kaidyn.

"At once. Those are our orders."

"Answer the question," Kaidyn told them. "Was it the Council who ordered this?"

"As requested to do so by Her Majesty Fianah Riverveil."

Kaidyn blinked. "Mother wants to see me?" He looked at

Sorin.

"Go," Sorin urged him, as if Kaidyn had the choice of refusing. "The quicker you are able to see her, the better."

Kaidyn nodded, allowing himself to be escorted to the waiting carriage without protest. The guards wasted no time in departing once he had seated himself inside. He leaned out the window to stare at the motionless figure behind as the carriage pulled away, watching Sorin grow smaller and smaller until he was nothing more than a still, dark shape under the approaching sunset. After that, Kaidyn simply closed his eyes and let the carriage bear him swiftly toward the palace, steeling himself for whatever was to come. The soldiers did not talk, even to one another, and he did not bother to look to them for answers.

He was doubly glad, later, of his composure—grateful for his years of training and practiced indifference that enabled him to stand with his back straight and his head held high. Facing his own sister in the throne room, he heard out her decree in silence, staring at the empty space where his mother should have sat. Only an hour or two before, Kaidyn had had hope. Now Lyrah spoke the words that the queen either would not or could not speak for herself, and Kaidyn knew they would be burned into his mind for as long as he lived.

"This war has drawn out long years, our soldiers stretched thin along our northern border. Yet the very people who should be helping them have remained aloof from the fighting for too long. Nor can we any longer afford to rely on volunteers to make up the dwindling numbers of our officers and soldiers. To live in our kingdom means to also serve our kingdom. You will tell your men that."

That Half-Bloods were now being ordered into soldiering rather than being paid volunteers dismayed but did not surprise Kaidyn. Anyone with an eye on Sareen's military or political affairs might have predicted that. More chilling was precisely where and how such men were to be deployed.

"A company will be sent north, to Fort Corlith. There, an Iskandirian company has captured the fort and taken up arms against us . . . alongside some of our fellow country-men." Lyrah's voice grew colder still. "*Former* fellow countrymen."

Fort Corlith. Kaidyn had heard the rumors of its loss to Iskandir forces but not been overly concerned by them, for even if it was true, it would have made little difference to the war for either kingdom. Corlith was small, little more than a far-flung outpost, and it had been poorly manned for years. Attempting to reclaim such an insignificant site would have been foolish, especially if doing so meant placing any sizea-ble number of Sareen's own men at risk.

That was one thing, and Kaidyn would have been angry but still resigned to his orders. But Half-Bloods fighting Half-Bloods . . .

He could spare no thought for his reply at first. "Do you hate me so much?" he asked his sister blankly. He saw the anger flicker in her eyes. "The men you order—demand *me* to order—have done nothing to deserve such treatment."

"Have they not?" Though clearly angry, Lyrah kept her calm. "Yet those Half-Bloods fighting against us are soldiers who abandoned their posts and now fight against the very kingdom that once sheltered them. Sareen took the risk of harboring potential traitors. This is how they have chosen to repay our trust."

"Perhaps if they had been better treated by Sareen, they would not have!" Kaidyn sought to rein in his temper, aware that it would do nothing to help his cause. "Regardless, you cannot judge the many based on the actions of a few. These men you order to arms are Sareen-born, this has been their home all their lives! They belong in this kingdom just as much as any who sit in this room," Kaidyn said more quietly. He looked around, but none of the Council would meet his eyes.

Lyrah did not raise her voice, but the stiffness of her posture betrayed her displeasure. "It is in part thanks to such idealistic views that this war has been allowed to draw out as long as it has. Half-Bloods have benefited from our kindness long enough. If this really is their home, they will all fight to defend it as ordered. It is time they repay their debt."

"You send good men to die for no purpose."

"I send men to do their job!" The rest of the Council was silent, their eyes carefully trained just above or to the side of Kaidyn's face. "Iskandir is a kingdom of fanatics and murderers, a race of people proclaiming Gifts to be base and evil. They've been killing their own for it for centuries, even attempting to execute their own king's own flesh and blood," she continued, as though pointing out the obvious to a child. "We would be foolish not to use every weapon at our disposal in order to defend ourselves."

Kaidyn had said nearly the exact same words to Sorin once, and was now sickened by them. "They — *we* — are not weapons, but flesh and blood," he countered.

"Yes. And as is our right, the Council now decides to have them do their duty. Just as it is my own duty to take necessary action in support of such a right."

"And such are the orders of Queen Fianah as well?" Kaidyn asked.

"I am here precisely to spare her from giving them!" Lyrah's sudden shout echoed around the near-empty throne room. A flush of embarrassment reddened her cheeks as the echoes died away. She took a moment to compose herself.

"It was mother who refused to hear the Council when they advised against her choices all those years ago," she continued more quietly. Her face might have been carved of marble, though her anger was still evident in the bite of her words. "Mother who refused to remarry when she finally became aware that those choices had been in the best interests of nobody but herself. Mother who stood by and did nothing for years, in the vain hopes that the war would simply come to an end of its own accord. Now she reaps the rewards. Since she has not the heart to deliver the orders in person, that duty too must fall to me."

Kaidyn waited for a moment before he spoke again, lest his voice lose its steadiness. "I ask once more," he said formally. "Is this my mother's decree? For I answer to nobody but the queen."

Lyrah gestured sharply, and a page boy standing near the door approached with a tray bearing a single parchment. "The queen's seal is fresh upon it for anybody who wishes to bear witness with their own eyes. These are her orders, not mine. For like you, brother, I merely act as my queen commands."

"Allow me to witness, then." Kaidyn did not believe his sister was lying, but he had to see for himself—had to look upon the words and know them to be true beyond a single doubt.

"I thought you would be better pleased," she told him, motioning for the page boy to hand over the document. "You will finally be allowed to prove your worth, just as you have always wished."

The ink was still dark and glossy on the page. "How long will I be given to train these men, and see them properly equipped?"

"You are to have twelve weeks."

That was nothing more than wishful thinking, and surely even Lyrah knew it. "Sister," Kaidyn said steadily. "Twelve months would not be sufficient to properly train and equip men who have never before held a sword in their hands. If the bulk of this company has been conscripted, then we are not talking of soldiers, but of servants and farmers.

"Those outside the capital will not have even twelve weeks, for even if they leave immediately, the journey may take days. More." He did not add the obvious—that as a newly appointed officer, he himself would be sorely lacking in experience. Yet as a trained officer, he would be expected to simply stand back and give the orders, and in doing so would likely live.

"I repeat. I am acting as my queen has commanded. As will you."

"May I see her?"

"You may not. Mother is indisposed and wishes to see nobody."

"I see."

And he did now. Kaidyn saw with startling clarity how such a thing had come to pass. His sister, the heir to the throne, was unquestionably loyal to the crown, but frustrated and ashamed by her own mother's refusal to take action on behalf of the kingdom and by the queen's lack of decisiveness despite her role as well. The queen herself was a woman who had never wanted that role and was much diminished by the losses she had suffered over the years. Her weakness no doubt served only to anger Lyrah further, working to turn frustration into bitter resentment.

It had nothing to do with hate, but even if it had, it scarcely mattered now. The decision had been made, and Kaidyn was aware that nothing he said would be able to change it. The fact that such a command would amount to little better than suicide for many suddenly conscripted men was beside the point. Lyrah was no fool, but she lacked any military experience—either she did not know the sheer number of lives that would be lost, or she had resolved not to care. Certainly nobody else would mourn the loss of a company of Half-Bloods.

So rather than protesting, finally letting loose all the things that he had wanted to shout at her since childhood, Kaidyn opened his mouth to speak the words he knew he must. He spoke them clearly and with as much dignity as he could muster, so that the entirety of the Council might hear them. His voice reverberated clearly in the otherwise near-soundless chamber.

"In that case, Your Highness, I will lead these men into battle personally."

CHAPTER TEN

Kaidyn did not know what to expect when he faced Luck for the first time since their argument months ago, but he had not expected an apology.

"Kai . . . I'm sorry. What I said to you—I was wrong." Even Luck's sun-darkened skin looked paler than usual, fresh bruises on his face standing out against his pallor. They were in one of the rooms directly overlooking the courtyard of his training school, which had now become the designated practice yard for the enlisted soldiers and newly conscripted men alike. Dusty and crowded with the constant arrival of men who had as yet been given no orders but to report in, it held an air of confusion and, on the faces of many, barely controlled panic. Kaidyn would have his work cut out for him.

"I should never've said any of it," Luck continued. "I spoke from anger. It was stupid of me."

"It's fine," Kaidyn said. He didn't feel angry at Luck any more. He didn't feel much of anything.

"No, it's not," Luck persisted. "I was an idiot and you were right to walk away like you did. I didn't even mean to say any of that, it's just . . . you were so—I was afraid of—"

"I know." And Kaidyn did. He of all people knew what hurt and jealously looked like.

They stared at each other until Luck stuck out his hand, still a little awkward. "Peace?"

Woodenly, Kaidyn extended his own hand for his best friend to clasp. "Peace," he agreed. But his heart was not in it.

It was not that he couldn't forgive Luck. He could, and he was keenly aware of what had driven Luck to lash out, fear and anger driving his words. After all, he had done the same more times in the past than he could be count. The dread of being alone, of being abandoned, was enough to bring about far more than a mere falling out between friends.

But from the minute he had left the throne room at the palace, seen Sorin turn white in shock and terror after Kaidyn had told him of what had come to pass there, it was as though he had grown numb to it all. He could spare energy for neither rage nor sorrow now, or even apprehension. The only emotions to penetrate the shroud that had stolen over him were concern for Sorin's well-being and the determination to see things through to their end.

"Almost funny to think it's finally come to this after so much time spent just waiting around for it." Luck gave a short laugh, but the sound held no joy. "We Half-Bloods — we always knew we'd never stand equal to anyone else. But I guess I just thought . . . hell, I don't really know what I thought. Not this. I knew them, Kai. Know them. We trained together. Now we're going to kill them. I thought we'd fight for something worthwhile, at least or that the Half-Bloods who weren't soldiers wouldn't have to fight at all. Just look at them. One minute they were going about their lives as farmhands or servants, and the next . . ." He gestured out at the milling throng and shook his head.

"Perhaps it was inevitable and we were only fools for not seeing it sooner." Kaidyn knew his words sounded hollow.

Luck frowned. "You were only supposed to train us. See us equipped and give us our marching orders. Yet I was told you volunteered to lead the company into battle yourself. Why?" he asked bluntly. "You could have spared yourself that, at least. Gods know you've never been one for heroics.

So why put yourself in this position?"

It was all but impossible to explain, even to himself. Still, Kaidyn made an effort to do so. "I had no other choice."

"What do you mean?"

"It's not just about me anymore," Kaidyn attempted to clarify. "Rather, it was never just about me to begin with. I was mistaken to ever think it was."

He could tell Luck didn't really understand, and he wasn't sure if he could fully comprehend it either. It was more than the urge to put the past behind him once and for all, to lay his personal demons to rest. Perhaps it was the need to make good on his word that had truly compelled him—the chance to help create a kingdom in which he and Luck and hundreds, maybe even thousands of others, could exist without prejudice or hatred. Such a chance would only ever be given to him once—even if that meant killing his own kind in exchange.

His mind shied away from the thought, even as he knew that it was so much bigger than him, so much larger than he'd ever imagined. Sorin's deepest wish was to see his vision of not only peace but also equality become a reality. Kaidyn wondered how such a future would come to pass if nobody was willing to fight for it. Now that he had dared to hope for such a future as well, he could not refuse to shoulder the responsibility for it, any more than his sister could refuse what she so plainly saw as hers.

"What did he say when you told him? Sorin, I mean. Can't imagine he was too happy with your choice."

Here was something Kaidyn could have explained more easily, but he could not bring himself to speak the words. How the shock had caused Sorin's voice to go faint as he murmured, almost inaudibly, "You swore you wouldn't leave me." He didn't know how to explain that he awoke time and time again to Sorin's screams with the sight of what only the gods knew causing him to panic until exhaustion overcame him. Kaidyn was utterly incapable of consoling him, holding his lover close until he fell asleep again but unable to tell him the one thing that would have given him peace — *I'll come back.*

It would have been a promise Kaidyn did not believe in, and he wouldn't betray Sorin that way — not even to bring him comfort. In turn, Sorin either would not or could not tell Kaidyn a word of what he saw in his visions, perhaps unwilling to distress him further, yet ironically only prompting him to worry more. And though Sorin did not say it, his haunted expression spoke the message clearer than words. He would have done anything to prevent Kaidyn from leaving. Anything at all.

But Kaidyn could not say this to Luck or anyone else. The words cut too close and too true. " . . . Not well," he replied finally, and Luck wisely changed the subject to something more practical.

"Right." He rubbed his hands together briskly. "We've twelve weeks to prepare ourselves. So what next?"

"We need to form groups for training. You know the enlisted soldiers better than I. Assign a sub-commander to each group. Make sure they're men you judge to be reliable."

Gods, but the task seems far bigger than I had ever imagined. The company he had been given was roughly the same size as the trainees he'd graduated with at the academy, yet he was only one person and many of these men were not even soldiers. They had been added to the ranks over the past few days. Most were half-grown boys more accustomed to wielding sickles or butcher's knives than swords. Some were men with graying hair past the age of service. Then there were the hotheads with too much courage and not enough caution. Many looked half-starved, most laughably inexperienced. Like Luck, plenty bore the marks of fighting with fists rather than swords. They might equally have been inflicted on each other as by anyone else.

Luck gave a noncommittal grunt. "We'd best get started then. I've some men in mind for the task."

Kaidyn nodded his assent and then remembered something else. "Luck. I have to ask you something. It's important."

Luck raised an eyebrow. "Not like you to sound so uncertain, even to me. Or should that be especially to me. What is it, Kai?"

"Me."

"What about you?"

There was no delicate way of putting it. "I'm not qualified to lead these men. To lead anyone at all, come to that. Why should they listen to me—an officer with no real experience, no first-hand knowledge of war? We might all be Half-Bloods, but most of them will only know me as the son of the queen. Why put their trust in someone like that?"

Luck snorted. "Simple. Because you can't possibly be worse than the people they've had lead them in the past."

"Luck, I don't—"

"And because you're still just like the rest of us," Luck interrupted, his expression growing more serious. "An unGifted half-breed and a threat to the kingdom as the rest of 'em know it. One of our own, a man worthy of respect. That's all there is to it in the end. We have our orders. There's nobody we'd trust more to see them out."

There could be no reply to this. No adequate one. Kaidyn tried anyway. "Luck . . ."

His friend made a face. "C'mon, don't play the tormented hero on me now. At least wait 'til we've got a couple of drinks down us first. But before that, there's a lot to be done. So let's get doing." He threw an arm around Kaidyn's shoulders. "We should start on drilling first, but after that, there's literally a whole stableful of horses already awaiting your inspection. Congratulations on your early promotion, by the way."

Luck's sardonic sense of humor was one thing that had not changed, at least. Kaidyn allowed himself to be led away, sinking gradually back into the dazed detachment that Luck had briefly managed to crack. He could not afford the luxury of giving any more thought to his own worries. There was no place for doubt, not in war—not even one he already knew, whether Sorin would tell him or not, that he was going to die in.

But not all had given into despair just yet. Kaidyn was in the midst of demonstrating a series of simple moves the following day when he suddenly froze, seeing a familiar figure walk through the gates of the training school. He was followed by several others, ordered and quiet.

"Lord Kaidyn." Emil grinned at him, apparently unbothered by the stares.

"I—what is—"

"You need help," said the other simply. "We're here to give it."

"We?" He turned to look again at the handful of men behind who had been his fellows at the academy, apparently waiting for Emil to direct them. All were dressed plainly and had practice swords at their hips. "But how did you—you can't just—"

"We can and we will." Emil put a friendly hand on his shoulder. "Most of us haven't been assigned to a regiment yet, so our time is still our own. And I don't recall there being any law that says noblemen and enlisted soldiers or conscripts are forbidden to fraternize, no matter their bloodlines." He waited for Kaidyn's still-stunned nod before beckoning the others forward.

Then it was a blur of several hours under a blazing sun as newly trained officers strode in and rearranged groups, distributing the trained soldiers more evenly. Kaidyn allowed Emil to direct the men and help them with their exercises. Most looked upon this small group of trained soldiers with predictable mistrust at first, but warmed to them as Emil and the others demonstrated many of the moves themselves rather than simply barking orders. They praised and hounded the men as necessary but did not patronize or bully them. When some men still questioned Emil's authority, he put them in their place with his sword, knocking them into the dust again and again until even the loudest were forced to respect it. By the end of the morning they were all sweating and exhausted, a ragtag company who were nonetheless finally grasping the idea of fighting as a unit.

Emil waited until Kaidyn had called a halt to rest and replenish themselves before approaching him again. They stood side by side, looking out over the training yard.

"You've some fine men here," Emil commented.

"Yet not even with the finest company in the kingdom would this battle be won without high cost. We are too few to recapture Corlith without losing at least half the company—and then we'd never be able to hold it without reinforcements should Iskandir attack a second time." Kaidyn's voice was bleakly matter-of-fact.

"True. But better to send trained men than mere street brawlers, soldiers rather than thugs."

Kaidyn looked down for a moment in embarrassment at this reminder of his own earlier behavior, though Emil did not dwell on it.

"We'll make soldiers out of them as best we may."

"Why send us at all?" It had been much on Kaidyn's mind, for even with his lack of experience as an officer, he could see no real advantage his company would win the kingdom. Fort Corlith meant nothing—even a victory would not bring the war any closer to an end.

"It is a good question." Emil regarded him quietly for a moment. "If I may speak plainly?" He waited for Kaidyn's nod of agreement. "It seems that the crown princess and the rest of the Council have all but assumed control over such matters, every one of them no doubt believing they act for the good of the kingdom. Certainly nobody questions the Council's loyalty, and Her Highness' decision is in many minds perfectly justified."

"You can't seriously be in support of such a ridiculous plan." A flicker of the old anger threatened to spark to life before Emil shook his head.

"I assure you, I am not. Nobody with any real military knowledge would approve it. I'm simply pointing out that the queen has her faults, just as anybody else. Everyone knows her to be tender-hearted, unwilling to lose good men—not necessarily the best of traits in a time of war, when sacrifices must often be made in exchange for victory. Hesitation to act in the past has cost our kingdom much. I'm only telling you what a lot of other people are thinking—that at least Her Highness, unlike the queen, is doing *something*."

Kaidyn was aware more than ever of his mother's short-comings but wanted instinctively to defend her. "How do you know this? You've never met either of them."

"I know because . . . look, I didn't want to say anything earlier lest it cause even more problems between us, but my paternal grandfather sits on the Council. And I'm telling you this not to anger you but because it might help you better understand. The queen's unwillingness to heed her Council on several occasions in the past has led to trouble elsewhere, maybe even helped prolong the war. Did you know she's not even attended the last few meetings, continually plead-ing fatigue or indisposition?"

" . . . I didn't," Kaidyn admitted in a low voice.

"Yet she forbade any action being ordered in her place.

The kingdom stood paralyzed for months. Now, for better or worse, she has finally chosen to stand back and allow others to make such decisions on her behalf. Who better suited to do so than her own daughter and heir?"

Kaidyn sighed, weary of politics. "This still does not explain why my sister has made this particular decision. What benefit does it bring?"

"From a military standpoint? Little enough that I can see," Emil answered frankly. "But the fort *is* within our borders, which we've a right and a duty to protect no matter how trivial the prize. And probably more to the point, there are plenty of people who would support such a move, no matter how much military sense in made. If it was not common knowledge before that a few of our enemy were once Half-Blood soldiers of Sareen, still in training or not, it is now."

It made a chilling kind of sense when Emil put it like that, but the thought brought Kaidyn no joy. He did not reply, but instead stared out at the men, now more relaxed and talking among themselves in small clusters. Some ate ravenously as bread was being distributed. A few were laughing at some joke. *How much longer do these men have? How much longer do any of us have?*

"Have you found an answer to my question yet?" Emil abruptly changed the subject, and it took Kaidyn a moment to be able to marshal his thoughts.

He shook his head. "No."

"Sure about that?" Emil looked at him, face serious. "I heard you volunteered to lead them into battle yourself. You bring them honor, my lord." And to his surprise, Emil bent his head in an unmistakable bow. "Though many may die, you do what you believe you must and for a purpose other than your own. *That* is a sword which can win against any other."

Kaidyn smiled a little mockingly at this, though he meant it for himself rather than at Emil. "I do what I must because I have no other choice."

"You're wrong." Emil was adamant. "There is always a choice. Run or fight, be branded a traitor or follow orders. Live or die." Emil's own smile was tinged with regret. "You've made yours. Now pick up your sword, Lord Kaidyn."

And Kaidyn did—because if he *was* going to die, he did not plan on doing so without first fighting tooth and nail to live.

Every day they trained until every man was exhausted, and every day Kaidyn felt the weather continuing to warm as spring turned into summer. The days turned into weeks, until there was but one night left before their departure. Time had finally run out—just as Sorin had probably always known it would.

That afternoon, standing one last time among the trees by the river, Sorin pleaded with him, trying to persuade Kaidyn to change his mind. Trying to get Kaidyn to *live*.

"You must not do this." Sorin's blue eyes were dark and wide, his skin chalky. He appeared almost in shock.

"I'm sorry."

"Please, you don't understand! It's all wrong, I've seen— don't do this!" Sorin's voice rose as he begged Kaidyn to stay, reaching out a hand to grasp his arm like he could forcibly keep him there. "I understand your reasons. I do! But please, you don't have to—they can't possibly—you *can't*—"

Kaidyn had never hated himself more than he did in that moment as he made himself remove Sorin's hand. He stepped back, schooling his expression to blankness. "I can and I must. You know this."

The hurt on Sorin's face at his coldness was plain to see. Still he continued to entreat Kaidyn. "You don't need to prove anything! Not to them! Not to anyone."

"Not to anyone else, that is true." Kaidyn took a breath, holding himself steady against the urge to hold Sorin in his arms just once more, to kiss him and refuse to let him go. But this was something Kaidyn could not allow to happen, and he told himself that the pain he was causing Sorin now was better than a promise he would not be able to keep. "Sorin, I'm not—"

"Don't! Just don't, Kai!" Sorin scrubbed a hand over his eyes, dashing away the tears that threatened to form. "What good is your dream if you die before it comes to fruition?" he asked desperately. "What good your honor if it means throwing away your life for people who care nothing for your vision of the future?"

"It means everything," Kaidyn answered honestly. "Sorin, I must do this. There's no other way. And if I should not come back, then at least I'll have—"

"No! I won't hear this." But Sorin's hand moved to cover his mouth rather than his ears, as though this action would somehow put a halt to his grief.

"Sorin . . ."

"No, just listen. Please." With an effort, Sorin steadied his voice. "All this time, you thought you were somehow lacking. That you were below everyone else, beneath them, even if you knew you did not deserve it. Beneath *me*. But you were wrong. And when you finally started to believe that you had something to offer the world . . . that you were worthy of respect, and of love . . . Kai, you swore to me an oath that you would not leave me and yet here you are—" He broke off, unable to continue, and it was almost impossible for Kaidyn not to close the gap between them again.

Almost. He forced his voice to indifference. Calm and remote—a stranger's voice—and prayed that Sorin would one day forgive him this. "I cannot stay. So what is it you would have me do, my lord?"

Sorin's head snapped up as he stared, hurt beyond words, at the man standing before him. But Kaidyn said nothing more, forcing Sorin to eventually find his voice again and break the terrible silence. "I would have you return to me," he whispered.

Kaidyn shook his head. "I can make no such promise."

The light would soon be fading. It was so quiet—that motionless hush between late afternoon and early evening. Kaidyn had chosen this place for its privacy and for what it meant to them both—the copse of trees that grew close to the river, their own charmed space where they had talked and laughed and loved. From here, one could look down and watch the freely flowing water or look up and see the wide open sky. Here one could lie on the grass and whisper small secrets or sleep with your head in another's lap. How odd that this place should appear so peaceful when the rest of the world was so violent. It was strange that the trees should appear so green, the sky so vividly blue.

Had it always been this beautiful?

" . . . When?"

Kaidyn glanced around at the gradually lengthening shadows. "We depart at first light." A single night, no more, which he must spend with his men in last-minute preparations and not with his lover in his arms.

They stood facing each other, wordless now, the stillness between them stretching out until it seemed ready to snap. Sorin clearly struggled to find some measure of composure while Kaidyn fought to maintain his aloofness, knowing that to give in to his longing and touch Sorin again would be to shatter into a thousand pieces. He must leave now while he still had the will to be so callous.

"It is time. There is still much to prepare."

"Wait!"

Kaidyn stopped, his back to Sorin, and heard Sorin walk

over to him. He trembled as Sorin moved to face him and took his hand, turning it palm-up and dropping something there before backing slowly away again.

Kaidyn looked down. "You cannot give me this," he said, his shock enough to crack the surface of his reserve. Sorin only ever removed his ring when he slept. The wood was still warm from where it had encircled his finger. Kaidyn kept his hand open, making no move to accept the token.

"It is mine to give as I see fit," Sorin said, "and I see fit to give it to you. You must either keep it or throw it away, for I will not take it back."

"Sorin—"

"No, do not argue." Now it was Sorin's voice that was cool. "Only return it to me when we see each other once more."

"I don't—"

"And when you do, marry me."

Kaidyn whirled around to stare at him. "I can't," he said, stricken.

"Say it."

"Sorin—"

"*Say it.*"

He paused and then bowed his head, defeated, as his hand curled around the ring to clench it tight. Sorin gave him no choice. "I will marry you, Sorin." He had not known before this moment that it was possible for a single body to hold so much bitter joy, so much exquisite pain.

"Then know that however long it takes, I will wait for you. I will always be waiting," Sorin told him softly. "Now go. Go quickly, before . . ."

Kaidyn obeyed. He did not look at Sorin again—did not dare, even once more, to glance behind him, lest his resolve turn to dust from the tears running freely down Sorin's face.

They rode out of the city as dawn broke, eyes staring straight ahead.

There was nothing resembling banter among the men now. Kaidyn knew they must paint a shabby picture. Their leather armor was plain and worn, and their weapons had clearly also seen better days. They were a motley group and likely pitifully mismatched — yet if they had a single similarity other than their tainted blood, it was that young or old, serving boy or seasoned veteran, all were determined to prove their loyalty to the one place they had ever called home.

But for all their courage, the streets were eerily silent. Custom dictated a sendoff that usually resembled something closer to a festival parade than a farewell. It was not auspicious to show either fear or sorrow when men went off to war. Children were supposed to throw flowers and wave streamers, sweethearts to wear bright colors and blow laughing kisses to the departing soldiers. The more noise that was made, the better, in order to chase away ill fortune.

Yet for all the people lining the road toward the main gates out of the city, the rising sun brightening their leave as was tradition, the gathering was subdued. When people spoke they did so in whispers, and they turned their faces away from those departing the capital, nobody quite willing to meet their eyes. Quiet, thick and heavy, lay over the city, and Kaidyn knew it for what it was — a pall of shame, though it should not have been theirs to bear. He wore Sorin's ring on a leather cord around his neck, hidden beneath his clothes, for he could not bear to wear it openly on his hand. Another mark of shame, this one deserved, since he knew it would soon mean a broken promise.

Still they rode and did not look back. Kaidyn did not search for Sorin's face anywhere among the crowd. He had resolved to remember it instead, not pale and drawn but the way it should have been, carefree and flushed with laughter.

He remembered it for the nearly two weeks it took to travel north across country, passing through foothills and woodlands, farms and villages. Each day, they traveled until darkness fell and his company lay quiet, either asleep or alone with their thoughts, feeling each passing hour as another step closer to an end. Then the sky would brighten again and they would continue onward, speaking little and pausing to rest only when they must, each man drawing what comfort they might from their memories. In the distance, Kaidyn once spotted the palace he had known in his youth, long deserted for its proximity to the border—and still he forced himself to remember Sorin's laughter and smile, all that day and the next, until the third morning afterward.

The day broke clear, with a fresh breeze that stirred the grass at his feet. The men assembled without fuss, though some horses sensed their tension and stamped their hooves, snorting uneasily. Kaidyn looked at them, resolving to remember not only Sorin but also the faces of those around him for as long as he could. He spoke something to Luck, to the rest of them, before gesturing their ranks forward, and the words vanished from his mind almost as soon as they had passed his lips. It was no grand hero's speech, but simply the best he could offer. War, after all, was not grand or honorable or dignified. War cared nothing for remembrance.

He thought he might have gone mad, then, and did not care. He heard things and saw things and tasted things that would only later come back to him in brief snatches—horses shrieking until they died, eyes rolling to the backs of their heads, the sun glinting off weapons of reddened steel as he swallowed past the blood in his mouth, his own sword cleaved to his hand as he became it, snarling and burning and screaming things he did not even know he could say.

For a time he burned hot and fierce enough that he had to chase them all down, for none would come near him as he roared and spat and cursed, unable to tell one man from another. He couldn't tell the difference when a fine red mist lay over everything, on ground, cloth, and armor. It was almost impossible to tell friend from foe when they all looked so alike. Yellow hair. Yellow eyes. His cries were theirs and theirs were his, and somewhere at the back of his mind he knew his mouth was open and that the inhuman roar was probably coming from him. Yet this knowledge, like everything else surrounding him, held no real meaning.

He fought until he remembered nothing else.

Then, beneath all that sound, a name. He paid it no heed, shaking his head to clear the blood from his eyes. Somebody had managed to cut him, he realized dimly, and lifted his sword again to slice open whoever had done so. The man — no, the boy — died at Kaidyn's feet, a look of stark horror painted on his face, as if it was Kaidyn he feared more than his own death. His eyes were still open, still staring at him from where he lay sprawled in the dust, the blood leaking from his skull. Kaidyn stared back until a scream jolted him back to his surroundings. He turned, howling his fury, to parry the blade that swung from somewhere behind him.

Kaidyn had thought his anger burned away, all his fury taken and assuaged because of Sorin. He had been wrong. It had only been waiting, lurking beneath the surface, and now that it had been set free it was more savage than ever. Kaidyn allowed it to consume him because he did not have anything else left to give. Very well then — he would give it his all until there was no more life within him to fuel it. The pain was not enough to make him stop, and nor were the bodies falling around him like threshed wheat, less still the repeated shouts of the name.

He did not know himself again until the agony of his

sword arm finally penetrated the haze, slowly draining him until he caught a glimpse of a figure cutting down another man beside him. The first man stopped, stumbled, righted himself at the last moment, his tightly curling hair plastered to his scalp.

"Get up," the man said urgently. "Kai, get up!"

He was on the ground, Kaidyn realized, and he was staring upward, not sure when or how he had come to be there. He groaned something as he was hauled back to his feet, thankfully from the left.

"You're heavy," he heard the man grunt.

"Luck . . ." Kaidyn knew him now. That was good. It meant he did not need to fight when his sword arm was useless and it suddenly hurt beyond reason to walk.

"We're getting out of here."

Kaidyn blinked. His mind moved sluggishly and his legs could not keep up with the rest of his body. He tried to pass his free hand over his face, but the movement was too much, and he gave a hoarse groan before lurching over, almost bringing Luck down with him. The jolt was enough to make the world blacken for a moment. Kaidyn gagged and retched, his fingers digging into the dampened earth.

"No you don't," Luck said angrily and jerked him up again. "I'm getting us out of this if I have to drag you all the way back home myself. Now get *up*, damn you!"

He didn't know why or how, but he obeyed. Luck was supporting nearly all of his weight and Kaidyn could taste vomit as well as blood, but step by step they were leaving the battlefield behind them.

There might have been other men beside them or merely his own footsteps Kaidyn was hearing. The sound of running horses could equally have been thunder in the distance. He didn't know, he didn't know anything, but Luck continued to drag him anyway, cursing him soundly when Kaidyn begged his friend to leave him there.

Then he was lying down again. The earth was moving but he was still—a blessing. The creak of wood and wheels. He tried to look out at the landscape he was leaving behind, but his vision was clouded now by smoke.

"What . . ."

"Fire," Luck said from somewhere beside him. He spat. "Bastards set the fort on fire rather than give it up."

"Then we need—"

"Let it burn. We're leaving this hellhole behind, much good may it do anyone." They both watched the column of dust and ash drift into the sky.

But with every inch of ground they covered, Kaidyn felt his body growing weaker. The sun beat down on him, making him pant and burn all over again. He spared a brief glance for his right arm, sprawled uselessly by his side, wondering if he was only imagining the part of the bone protruding from the grisly mess of severed skin and muscle tissue. His vision was growing hazy, and he wasn't sure if it was because his eyes were swollen shut or if they were only congested with fluid. He tried to speak when he could no longer make out the figure of Luck beside him, but could only manage some kind of garbled cry as the ground rolled and the sky spun and his blood stained the hard surface beneath him.

Later—a minute, an hour, a day or maybe more—there were words in his mind, not his own, but a question being asked of him. Kaidyn felt a reply bubbling to his lips but his voice failed him. He gave up and lay still instead, listening to the call of his name.

Kai!

It might have been close. It might have been real. It might have been Sorin. There was no way to tell.

Kai!

He only wished he had the strength to remember Sorin's face again, one last time. But he did not, and so he closed his eyes.

CHAPTER ELEVEN

Water.

He didn't hear it this time, but he could feel the coolness on his dry, cracked lips, and when he licked them he tasted it too—and when he did that he knew the voice again.

Kai . . . Kai, wake up, love. I know you're still with me. Now open your eyes and look at me. I'm right here, so come back to me . . . come back . . .

For a moment he struggled against it, because it hurt to become aware of things again, but something about the voice gnawed at him until his body had time to remember. By the time the pain shot through him it was too late to turn back—his eyes had already snapped open.

Sorin was a figure clad in red and gray. No, Kaidyn corrected himself, only in gray. He had never seen him in the healer's uniform before, worn on the battlefield so that none might mistake him for a soldier and cause him harm, but it was spattered with blood. Kaidyn moved his mouth, trying to form the question. "Are you . . . hurt?"

"It's not my blood." Sorin's own eyes stood out against the rest of his face, wide and afraid. Kaidyn would have touched him if he could have, but Sorin was holding him down. "Don't move," he instructed shakily. "I have to clean the wounds, they're festering."

Kaidyn immediately knew this to be a lost cause. "Don't. Just . . . talk. Want to hear . . . your voice," he managed, and Sorin gave the ghost of a smile.

"You may listen to me to your heart's desire later. For

141

now I have to heal you, and that means no talking."

"Sorin, stop!" Nora's voice was a whip crack, sharp and commanding. Kaidyn had not even noticed her until now and wondered vaguely who else was nearby, how much time had passed — *hours? days?* — but then abandoned the thought, not caring. "I don't need to tell you what will happen if you proceed with this foolishness!" she continued.

"I can do it, Nora."

"I do not doubt your skills or your resolve, but there are some things beyond even the most powerful of Gifts."

"This is not beyond mine," Sorin argued, sounding desperate.

"Know your limits, you stubborn idiot!" Nora snapped at him.

"You're wasting precious time! I said I can do it, now leave us alone!"

Kaidyn did not think he had ever heard Sorin shout in anger before.

"And I'm telling you, you can't! Against my advice you've already exhausted your body to the point of doing it real damage, now stop before it's too late —"

"I said *leave*!"

"Kaidyn would not want you to die!"

There was a ringing silence. With an effort, Kaidyn kept his eyes open as Sorin turned to look at him again. He didn't say a word, but his face was asking a question. Slowly, Kaidyn moved his head to the side — once, twice. *No.*

"Don't . . . die . . ."

"I won't," Sorin pleaded, and Kaidyn smiled.

"Then say . . . good . . . bye . . ."

"Please don't leave me," whispered Sorin.

"Time . . ."

"Not yet!"

Kaidyn made himself stare past Sorin at a figure he assumed to be Nora, hoping she could read on his features what he wanted to say, for he had no breath left to speak it.

"Sorin. Kaidyn is right. It's time. There is nothing you or anyone else can do for him now. Allow him this. Allow him *peace.*"

When Sorin didn't move, Nora took him by the hand and tried to pull him away, but he shook her off. "Leave us alone," he said again, this time in a whisper.

"Sorin—"

"I wish to speak my farewells in private! Please . . . just go . . ."

Nora looked as if she might argue, but Kaidyn made some kind of noise—he didn't know what—and watched Nora back down.

"I'll be waiting outside," she said quietly.

Then there was only Sorin, gazing down at Kaidyn like he was about to cry, and Kaidyn could not even lift a hand to stroke his face.

"I don't want you to die," Sorin said, voice broken.

"Ready . . ." Kaidyn couldn't tell how he forced the word out, the blood bubbling from between his lips. But the pain was at least starting to fade again, his right arm gone nearly numb. He thought the sodden bandage might be the only thing still attaching it to his body, and felt glad Sorin wasn't looking at it now.

"I'm not," he replied, and Kaidyn had to think for a moment before he could assign meaning to the words or recollect what they had been in answer to. "I'm not ready, Kai!" Sorin's hand tangled in the strands of Kaidyn's blood-crusted hair, the other balled into a fist by his side.

He remained that way for a time, wordlessly stroking him as Kaidyn dutifully watched. He didn't want to stop watching until the very last second, though the darkness gathering at the edges of his visions was warm and not unwelcome.

Gradually, the tension leaked from Sorin until he stopped shaking and leaned down, heedless of the filth or the smell—sweat and vomit and rotting flesh—to kiss Kaidyn's brow. He bent his head lower so that his mouth was close to Kaidyn's ear. "Close your eyes again," he murmured. "Just for a while. I promise."

If he went to sleep then he wouldn't wake up again, Kaidyn thought fuzzily. But the darkness was pulling at him, soft and insistent.

"That's right. Didn't I say I would wait for you? I can wait a little longer."

Kaidyn frowned at that. A lifetime was a long time to wait. Too long. Sorin shouldn't have to do so on his account. His love should live and be happy with someone who was still alive to love him back.

"It's all right. You can let go now if you like. Just like that. Go to sleep."

Sleep was inevitable, whether Kaidyn wished it or not. He felt himself relax, giving in to the tide and slowly being swept away. It wasn't cold. The water welcomed him, like easing into a bath after a long day. It would close around his aching body, make him clean again. That was good.

I love you.

It was enough to know it.

Kaidyn was floating.

His body felt cradled, weightless, as though suspended in water or air. There was no form to it—it merely was, and Kaidyn existed somewhere within it.

This small awareness tickled at him but did nothing to interrupt his sense of calm. It was a rather pleasant sensation, if slightly odd, and there seemed no reason to pay it much heed. It felt not unlike hovering between sleep and wakefulness, but with nothing pulling him in one direction or the other. It felt good to simply lie there and allow himself to drift, slow and languid.

After a time, he grew curious enough to open his eyes.

There was no shape to Kaidyn's surroundings, nor even any color, but this did not strike him as being disconcerting. It was only as though there was no physical thing to be seen other than Kaidyn himself.

That thought sparked another, and he glanced vaguely down at his right shoulder. He couldn't think why, but he had expected to see something different about the limb, and was a little surprised when it was the same as he remembered. He raised his sword arm, testing it out, and then let it fall back to his side as he sat up to look over the rest of his body.

Kaidyn realized he was naked, but like everything else, this fact did not seem to matter. Although he was sure he had been wearing some sort of clothing earlier, this was a memory that was somehow blurry around the edges. He wasn't sure what type of clothes he had been wearing exactly and when, or even why he had been wearing them—such details felt as if they had come from a dream.

"Or perhaps I am dreaming now?" Kaidyn wondered aloud.

"Yes."

"Sorin!" He smiled a welcome. Here was something that could never be forgotten, not after a thousand nights of endless dreaming. "I am glad to see you safe," Kaidyn told him. This felt important, though he could think of no reason why Sorin should not have been so.

"As I am you," Sorin replied. "I was worried."

"Oh." Kaidyn thought, trying to remember. " . . .Why?"

"Don't you know?"

"No," Kaidyn admitted after another moment of thought. "Sorin, why are we here?"

"We are waiting, I think. Both of us at the same time, and

so we are able to meet here like this."

"I see." He didn't really, but Sorin did not seem alarmed or upset, so Kaidyn saw no reason to be either. "I feel fine," he added as an afterthought, casting a glance over himself again. Sure enough, there was not a scratch to be seen.

"Me too," Sorin said and Kaidyn saw how serene his companion looked, how happy. His hair, clean and glossy, hung freely down past his shoulders just like it had on the day they first met, and the dark blue of his eyes was deeper and clearer than Kaidyn had ever seen them. There were no marks of exhaustion on his face, no weariness or sorrow reflected there. Sorin appeared almost to glow from within, his very being radiating health and contentment.

"You are beautiful," Kaidyn murmured, reaching for him, and Sorin slipped easily into his arms.

"So are you," Sorin sighed happily although there was a twinge of wistfulness to his voice. "I wish we could stay like this forever."

Kaidyn blinked. "Why can't we?"

"Because nothing is forever," Sorin reminded him. "And because in a while I must go, no matter how much I might wish otherwise."

At these words, a jolt of foreboding broke through the stillness. "Don't leave!" Kaidyn implored him, then felt a flare of distorted déjà vu that swiftly faded when he tried to chase it down. He couldn't make sense of some of what Sorin had just said, but knew above all that he did not want him to go. *If Sorin leaves — if he goes away now —* Kaidyn was not quite able to complete the thought, but it awoke in him a jarring sense of unease.

"I will not have a choice, love," Sorin responded, pressing their foreheads together comfortingly.

He had called Kaidyn that before, though Kaidyn couldn't recall when. That was another thing that felt strangely important—something that needed to be remembered, and quickly. He paused, thinking hard, attempting to pin down the stray piece of information.

Sorin's kiss was distracting. "You need not worry about it," he said when he broke away to look at Kaidyn again. "For you there will be time enough later. I know it."

"What about you?"

Sorin shook his head. "I don't think so. But that's all right. I've done what I needed, so it's not important."

"That's not—wait!" Kaidyn recollected something in a flash of cold like ice down his back. "*I* was the one who was supposed to leave!"

" . . . I know. I'm sorry."

"No! I can't—you don't have to—"

"It was my choice," Sorin assured him. "Mine and mine alone."

"That's not the point! You were meant to stay! I beg of you, don't do this!"

"It's already done, love." The cloud that had passed briefly over Sorin's face at Kaidyn's pleas lifted, and the return of his smile was like the sun emerging. "Kai, you need to know that there is nothing I would have done differently. I don't regret a thing—not then and not now. This is the path I chose for myself. Whatever happens, whatever anger or guilt you might feel, you must remember that. Promise me that you will."

"No . . . this is all wrong, it wasn't meant to happen this way . . ." Kaidyn gripped Sorin's shoulders, afraid to lose him.

"Perhaps it was." Sorin gazed at him, still peaceful in the face of Kaidyn's rising disquiet. "I have waited all my life to feel like this but never once believed it could come to pass. Not for me. The sacrifice was necessary in the end. I truly believe that, Kai."

"I don't know what you mean," Kaidyn said, imploring. "Sorin, I don't want this! Can't you do anything to stop it?"

Sorin shook his head. "That is impossible now," he said gently.

"But I love you!" Kaidyn hugged Sorin to him, unwilling to let go, but something was happening. Sorin was diminishing, growing lighter and more insubstantial in Kaidyn's arms by the second. No matter how Kaidyn tried to keep him there, Sorin kept slipping away like water through fingers.

"Sorin . . . no, please gods no. Don't — "

"Kai. It's all right," Sorin said and pressed his lips to Kaidyn's once more, firm and sweet. That kiss utterly disarmed him, just as it always had, and Kaidyn let his arms fall to his side, defeated. He watched as Sorin began to vanish before his eyes and felt the tears well up, but Sorin saw them and shook his head again.

"Don't cry, Kai. Don't be sad — not now. I know you might not believe this, but we might even meet again someday."

"How could I not be sad?" Kaidyn whispered.

"Can't you tell?" Sorin was barely visible now, little more than a rapidly fading shape in the perfect nothingness surrounding them, but his last smile was one of joy. "I'm finally free."

Kaidyn awoke to the sound of the rain. He thought it was a part of his dream at first, for it had been so long since he had heard such a sound, but it became stronger as he drifted back to wakefulness. It drummed around him in a distant rhythm, growing closer and louder with every breath.

He lay still with his eyes closed a few moments more, gathering the shreds of his awareness and weaving them back together until he could make sense of things again. His body felt heavy but painless, and he was lying on his back beneath something soft. Somebody was sitting very close to him. He knew this because he could hear them quietly weeping. Kaidyn's dream was already fading from memory, and he could no longer remember anything but the haziest of details. Sorin had been there, they had spoken, but beyond this he had little recollection.

Still silent, he opened his eyes.

It was either very late or very early; there was no light from the window filtering into the room and no sound he could detect from beyond it. The dark shape by his bedside blurred, Kaidyn's vision adjusting to the dimness of the candlelit chamber until he could eventually make out the figure of his mother. She was bent so that her head rested in her hands, her hair loose and puddling to the floor. Her cries were soft, almost inaudible, and Kaidyn wondered whether the tears were of sorrow or relief.

Still blinking off the vestiges of sleep, he reached out a hand to touch her. "Don't cry, mother," he said, voice husky with disuse, and she startled and lifted her head to stare at him, the droplets still clinging to her eyelashes. "I'm—"

"Kaidyn!" She threw her arms around him before he could say anything more, pressing him to her as though he was a child again.

Kaidyn found he did not mind. He stayed still and allowed her to cry into his hair, clinging to him until her sobs eventually died away.

He felt he should apologize, though he could not quite remember for what. "Mother, I'm s—"

"No!" Her arms squeezed him tightly. Don't say it, Kaidyn, not to me! Not when I could not—when I did not . . ."

"It's all right," Kaidyn said. He still felt dazed, unsure of what had passed or why.

His mother shook her head. "No." she said again. The

word was quieter now, though her mouth still trembled. "The things I did, the things I failed to stop — oh Kaidyn, you lay so still for days, you looked . . . Nora insisted you would live, yet I could not bring myself to believe even that, not after . . ." She shook her head again, unable to finish. "Forgive me," she whispered.

Kaidyn took proper stock of the room as his mother blinked hard and made an effort to compose herself, wiping at her eyes with her fingers. This was the palace, he recognized with a start. Not the one in the capital, but the northern palace in which he had spent most of the first years of his life. This bedchamber had once been his own as a young child, though it looked far smaller than he remembered.

"I'm alive," he confirmed quietly, not really understanding why he said it but surprised nonetheless by the knowledge. He had not expected to see this place again, or his mother for that matter, or even —

"Sorin!" Kaidyn shot up with a gasp. "Where is Sorin?" He glanced around wildly, as though the room itself would give him the answer he sought.

"Kaidyn . . ."

"Where is he?" he demanded, and his heart was thumping so hard that all the air was being driven from his chest.

The queen drew back a little at the note in his voice. "Here, in the palace. But he . . . Kaidyn, I'm so sorry. He isn't . . ."

" . . . Is he all right?"

The question was not really a question, for Kaidyn remembered now. He remembered Sorin looking down on him, on his broken form and being told that saving him was a lost cause. But Sorin had somehow done it anyway. Heedless of what Nora had said, ignoring her warnings, Kaidyn had been healed, which meant Sorin must have exhausted every spark of his energy to do so, even though Kaidyn had already said his goodbyes. He was *here*, and so Sorin . . .

. . . Sorin could not be.

The awareness hit him full force and he struggled to breathe through it, making himself finish the thought.

Kaidyn had been prepared to die, and Sorin had sacrificed himself anyway.

Sorin was dead.

Sorin is dead.

He sat frozen, preparing himself for the words he knew he would hear from his mother's lips.

"He's alive."

The reply was so unexpected that Kaidyn was not sure he had heard correctly. "He — what?"

"Sorin is alive," the queen repeated. "Nora is with him now. He is sleeping." But she did not sound happy. She was looking at Kaidyn with both love and pity in her gaze.

"He is . . . wounded, then?" Kaidyn asked carefully. "But how?"

"Not wounded," his mother shook her head. "Nora cannot tell me why — only that he will not wake."

Kaidyn's hands clenched. "How long has he been asleep? It's normal for him to be unconscious a while after healing a serious injury, I must have been near death when he got to me, there's nothing so unusual about —"

"Kaidyn," his mother gently interrupted him. "Nora knows all this. She does not believe that Sorin will return to us."

"If he is alive then there must be a reason," Kaidyn argued desperately. "He wouldn't still be here, if . . . there would be no *point* in his still being alive, if he wasn't going to . . ."

The queen reached out to place her hands on top of Kaidyn's own, and her wrists were thin enough that he could feel every bone as she squeezed. "I know you care for this man very much," she said, when her son had eventually fallen silent. "I wish I could tell you what it is you want to hear. But I cannot."

Kaidyn stared down at the coverlet. "I want to see him."

"Oh Kaidyn, I don't think—"

"I want to see him."

But as he stood next to the bed some time later, looking down at Sorin's unmoving form and trying to deny the proof of his mother's words, Kaidyn knew she had spoken only truth. Sorin was too still, too quiet. It was as if, despite being otherwise in apparent perfect health, his spirit had flown, leaving only an empty shell behind.

"He has been like this since we found him, collapsed beside you," Nora told him. She spoke quietly despite the fact that she had assured him Sorin would not stir.

"Tell me."

She looked at him in much the same way as his mother had. "Kaidyn, this isn't—"

"*Please.*" He had to know.

" . . . I came back to check on Sorin when he did not emerge after several minutes. He was pressed closely against you, his arms around your body. Both of you were already unconscious."

"Why did you not stop him?" Kaidyn asked hollowly, trying his best not to sound accusing.

"Had such been possible, I would have. But severing Sorin's connection with you would have been like severing a thread. You were bound to each other through his Gift. Had I interfered then, I would almost certainly have killed you both."

"I see."

But he didn't. He didn't see at all. It seemed utterly pointless to have Sorin miraculously live through that, only to be dead in all but name. He appeared near-perfect to Kaidyn—

too thin by half, yet his skin was a healthy pink and unmarked. Despite the relaxed expression on his face, however, Kaidyn knew that for every moment Sorin slept on, it became less and less likely he would eventually wake. For every breath he took, he would fade away from them a little more, his body weakening until he would finally breathe his last. Pointless, and unimaginably cruel.

"How long until . . ."

Nora knew what he was asking. "A while yet, but this cannot go on forever. We've managed to make him drink a little, but it's not enough. He'll die without food, Kai."

"There's nothing you can do?"

But Kaidyn already knew the answer before Nora opened her mouth. If there was any way of waking Sorin, she would already have done so.

In the quiet that followed, Kaidyn reached up to unfasten the leather cord from his neck and slip the ring back onto Sorin's finger.

The sun rose and set and rose again, and Kaidyn rarely left Sorin's side.

He occasionally had company. Several times his mother came to sit beside him, as did Luck with a pronounced limp to his walk and a bandaged left eye. He would have some dashing new scars to show off to the ladies, he claimed, though Nora had declared his sight would not be affected, and that the leg would heal itself in time. She and the other healers had their work cut out for them with more serious wounds, for the palace had been transformed into a makeshift infirmary.

Most of the beds were little more than straw pallets over which old and musty linens had been placed. The palace had not been occupied in many years, and the furnishings, or at least those that were left, were ragged with neglect. Supplies from the capital arrived slowly. Still, neither Nora nor any-one else complained. They went about their jobs as best as they could, stepping through rooms crowded with rows of patients.

The northern palace was bustling, however, not only with wounded soldiers and messengers but also with the arrival of even more pressing news. Many other soldiers were mak-ing their way to the palace from where they had been posted all along the northern border, for the old king of Iskandir had been proclaimed dead. His heart, it was said, had finally succumbed to years of increasingly heavy drink, among oth-er, more dangerous vices. Iskandir had no queen, and so the king's oldest son had ascended the throne, publicly calling for an end to the hostilities. The war, it seemed, was finally drawing to a close.

This knowledge should have been momentous. The entire kingdom was no doubt abuzz with it. Yet callous as it felt, Kaidyn could not bring himself to care. In the face of so many lives lost, and of Sorin slipping further and further away from him with every passing moment, Sareen's so-called victory left him with only a gaping emptiness.

Kaidyn heard much of the news from Luck, who had been oddly quiet over the past days but was now impatient to leave.

"Did Nora already declare you fit to travel?" Kaidyn asked him.

"I wasn't about to check. Nobody's been discharged yet, but who knows how long that could take." He clapped Kai-dyn on the shoulder. "Do you want me to stick around a bit longer? I could make myself useful around here a while more, help out the wounded . . ."

"Where would you go otherwise? Back to the capital?"

"Gods no. South. As far away from the capital as I can get. I've a friend who says he might be able to find me a job.

Honest work as a stablehand. I've had more than enough of playing the warrior."

"Oh." Kaidyn did not begrudge him that. If there was any peace to be found for the men who yet lived after fighting alongside him, he would urge them to take it.

Luck read the message in his eyes. "You're not leaving yourself, then."

"No. Not until . . ."

"I know."

They sat in silence until the door opened again and Nora shooed him out, though she did not attempt to talk Kaidyn into leaving. Despite being able to do nothing to help, she had been a regular visitor at Sorin's bedside, though the steady procession of other patients meant she could never stay for long.

"Are you angry with me?" Kaidyn asked Nora once.

Nora didn't ask what Kaidyn meant. "No. For better or worse, this is the path Sorin chose. I cannot blame you for it." She gave him a frank stare. "And you should not blame yourself, either. Whatever happens, you must not let guilt darken your path ahead. Sorin has given you your life. Do not squander it."

And so time marched onward, and Kaidyn stopped counting the days as they passed. It continued to rain—a light but steady downpour that had not let up by the time his mother came to find him again.

At the queen's firm insistence, Kaidyn had left Sorin's room for some fresh air. It was be the first time he had been outside the palace at all since his arrival. He had seen his mother only in passing since he had woken. By day she made herself busy, fetching and carrying as though she was of no more importance than a serving girl. When darkness fell, the candles in her chamber burned long into the night as a small contingent of attendants came and went, laden with ink and parchment. Only once had he come across her in a moment of stillness, pressed closely to Nora on a bench overlooking the garden in one of the courtyards. They were quiet, their eyes on the gathering evening, and did not notice Kaidyn. He left them like that, two dark heads leaning against one another in mutual comfort, retreating in silence lest he disturb their rare moment of peace.

Now Kaidyn stood staring out at the same courtyard—a smaller version of the one in the capital. The garden was long overgrown, choked with old weeds and bramble, but peeking shyly out among them were scraps of color, bright against the gray of the sky.

It was just as beautiful as Sorin had once imagined it to be.

Kaidyn turned at the sound of footsteps approaching him. With none of her usual advisers in residence, it appeared nobody dared rebuke the queen for refusing to appear the part. Her hair hung unbound and undressed, her bare feet damp with soil and a ring of dirt around the hem of her gown.

"Mother, I—what is it? Is it Sorin?" he asked sharply, seeing her expression.

She nodded, reaching out to hold him by the wrist as he attempted to dash past her. "Kaidyn, wait! Listen to me a moment. Nora is with him now. Your young man, it seems, is finally awake, but . . .Nora won't say what, but something is not as it should be. She has requested that nobody disturb her while she looks over him—no, not even you," she said, as Kaidyn made to interrupt. "Kaidyn, it sounds most grave. Whatever it is, my son, whatever has happened . . ."

She dropped his hand at the look on his face, and Kaidyn ran past her. He didn't care. Sorin was awake. Nothing in the world could possibly be of more importance than this.

The door to Sorin's chamber was shut and barred from

within. It was torture for Kaidyn to stand there, employing every shred of restraint in his possession simply to wait. He soon gave this up in favor of restlessly pacing, unable to keep still. He heard Nora murmur something. His heart beat painfully hard at the sound of Sorin's voice replying, though Kaidyn could make out none of the words.

It might have been hours before the door finally cracked open. Nora did not look surprised to find Kaidyn standing there, his silence all but screaming his needed to be allowed admittance.

But Nora would not let him pass right away. She blocked the door with her body and looked up at him, her face carefully neutral. "You can go in soon but—Kaidyn, just look and listen to me first! This is important. Sorin is awake, but things cannot be exactly as they were—"

"It does not matter to me," Kaidyn interrupted, impatient.

"It will to him," Nora tried to warn, but Kaidyn could not wait a single moment longer. He pushed her aside and if Nora said anything more, he did not have the ears to hear. The door finally closed behind him as, trembling in nervous excitement, Kaidyn approached the bed at the far end of the chamber.

Sorin was sitting up, his knees drawn into his chest. A bowl of some kind of soup, only half-emptied, sat on the table beside him as he stared out the window. He shifted slightly at the sound of Kaidyn's footsteps, although most of his face remained turned away, his expression hidden.

"Sorin?" Kaidyn could not stop his voice from shaking. "Gods, I'm so glad . . .so glad . . ." Dizzy with relief, he fell to his knees beside the bed, fighting to keep himself from laughing or crying or both, or from clutching Sorin to him without another thought.

Kaidyn might have done all these things had he not realized even as he spoke that something was indeed amiss. For all Kaidyn's joy at seeing Sorin alive and well, Sorin held himself stiffly and would not turn to face him. Kaidyn hesitated, wanting to reach out but suddenly unsure of how Sorin's might react.

"What is it? Are you in pain?"

Mutely, Sorin shook his head.

"Are you sure? You seem . . ." *Distant*, he wanted to say, and after a moment Sorin finished the sentence for him.

"Different?" It was the first word to pass his lips, and his voice sounded strained, almost harsh—so unlike himself that Kaidyn's relief at hearing him speak was overtaken by apprehension.

"What is it?" he asked again, pleading. "What can I do?"

"Nothing. There's nothing you can do." Sorin was usually so easy to read, so open, but Kaidyn could not pinpoint the emotion behind his words now.

" . . .Do you hate me for what I've done?" he ventured, dreading the reply.

"*No!*" Sorin's reaction was immediate and emphatic. "Never," he continued more calmly, and Kaidyn knew he would not lie to him. "I would never blame you, Kai. This was my choice and no other's."

Never blame him for what? Sorin was scaring him now. "Then tell me, please," Kaidyn entreated, urgent.

"I . . .Kai, promise me you won't . . ." Sorin didn't seem capable of finishing and was still refusing to look at him.

Not knowing what else to do, Kaidyn gave in to the urge to touch. He brushed his fingers lightly against Sorin's face.

Sorin flinched back.

Kaidyn drew in a breath, struggling not to show his hurt. "Sorin, please, look at me," he begged. "Tell me what's wrong."

When Sorin did not respond, Kaidyn reached out once

more to touch him. This time his fingers rested hesitantly on his lover's hand. He kept them there when Sorin made no move to pull away, waiting for Sorin to make up his mind.

Slowly, so very slowly, Sorin turned toward him.

But something was still not right. Sorin was looking at Kaidyn, but at the same time not looking at him at all. His eyes were pointed toward Kaidyn, yet they stared straight past him, through him, like he wasn't even there. As though Sorin couldn't—

"No," Kaidyn whispered as the truth finally dawned on him. "No, oh no, Sorin—" Those blue eyes were as dark and as beautiful as ever, but still—

"I'm sorry, Kai. I'm so sorry—" Sorin's voice caught on the words. He began to apologize over and over again, fingers tightly clenched, begging for forgiveness even though none of it was his fault. His words ran together until Kaidyn finally gave up on trying to stop him and simply pulled Sorin in close instead, his mouth against his lover's fine black hair. Kaidyn waited for him to calm, to say what he now already knew.

"I can't see."

Kaidyn's arms only tightened about Sorin in response.

Outside, the rain finally stopped.

CHAPTER TWELVE

"It's so blue today. There are only one or two clouds in the sky. There's one right above you shaped like a running horse."

Sorin lifted his face toward the sun, sighing appreciatively as the breeze ruffled through his hair. "It is a good day for this." His hand tightened on Kaidyn's arm—not because he was anxious or needed any assistance balancing himself, Kaidyn thought, but simply because he wanted to.

On his other side, Kaidyn bore a basket filled with soft bread freshly baked from town, several early season apples, small but pleasantly tart, and a skin of honeyed wine. "A perfect day for our first afternoon back at the river," he agreed.

Sorin tilted his head slightly, listening. "I think I can already hear the water."

Kaidyn fell silent but could hear nothing beyond the sound of their footsteps as they walked, the wind rustling every now and again through the trees. The river was still some distance away, but it would not have surprised him if Sorin had indeed already caught the faraway rushing of the current.

Sorin was beginning to rely on his other senses more and more, and his hearing seemed to be growing especially acute. He was showing a similar adeptness for being able to focus on the small, subtle noises that other people tended to miss, tuning out those sounds that were louder or closer in order to hear beyond them.

160

This did not mean that the past several weeks back in the capital had been easy ones.

Time and time again, Kaidyn had seen Sorin choke back tears of frustration as he was forced to relearn how to do all the things he had once taken for granted. The simplest of tasks had been transformed into a series of sometimes agonizing challenges, from dressing and eating by himself to walking unaided through his own home.

Kaidyn helped as much as he was able, but he did not wish to crowd Sorin or injure his pride. Sorin was a quick study and had always held a certain gracefulness, but it was difficult for Kaidyn to remind him to be patient as he fumbled awkwardly with the buttons of his shirt or slopped water over himself when he poured a drink. It was even more difficult for Kaidyn not to rush to Sorin's side when he misjudged the distance from the door to the bed and bruised himself on the furniture, or when he tripped and fell to the ground after attempting to walk the palace courtyard with neither his hand pressed to the wall for balance nor Kaidyn leading him by the hand. These days were difficult, exhausting, and punishing on both body and spirit.

Kaidyn had also grieved — was still grieving — for the men who had perished under his command as well as for those he had put to the sword. Half of his company had died for the sake of a minor fortification that had been burned to the ground, while at least some of those Kaidyn had killed had once been men of Sareen — men like himself. He felt both sorrow and anger for their betrayal, along with some understanding and a terrible sense of loss for what might have been. Unable to express these feelings to anyone else, he sought comfort in Sorin's arms, just as Sorin sought solace in return.

Neither was Kaidyn's time entirely his own. He visited the palace when he could, knowing his mother was still working day and night, determined to repair the damage that had been done to the kingdom over the course of many years of war. By royal decree, the Council had been indefinitely dissolved, with the queen now seeking advice from individual men and women whom she felt she could personally trust.

Meanwhile, Lyrah trailed behind the queen like a pale shadow, listening much and speaking little. Kaidyn did not know what words the pair had exchanged, or if his sister had received any kind of formal punishment for her actions. Still, her demeanor was somber. *Has she come to realize just how much she must grow before she is able to rule fairly as well as skillfully? Just as I myself needed to grow when I first met Sorin?* And so the season bled into high summer, the stress of it all often challenging to bear.

But for all the pain and frustration of the past weeks, there was joy and laughter, too. It was finally over — not only the war, but also all the fear and dread that had led up to it. Kaidyn and Sorin were now both free in a way that had never before been possible, and they reveled in each other's company. With nothing to darken their way ahead, their spare time was filled with unhurried embraces and periods of quiet in which no words were needed.

Privately, Kaidyn also wondered whether a part of Sorin was secretly relieved. He had not said as much, but Kaidyn knew without needing to ask that his lover's sleep was untroubled, liberated from the kinds of visions that had haunted him all his life. In their place, he had been granted a peace of mind that he had once thought to be unobtainable, and Sorin's contentedness was plain to see in every undisturbed night of slumber, every glowing smile, every lingering touch. Meanwhile, his Gift of healing seemed to have grown even stronger.

Kaidyn could hear the low roar of the river now as they approached their accustomed spot on the bank. More rainfall had caused the river to swell, making its currents swift and too dangerous for swimming, but they settled themselves near a cluster of trees and relaxed. Alone in one another's company, they ate and drank their fill, passing the wine between them and feeling their bodies grow warm and lazy in the sun.

Sorin leaned against Kaidyn's side after they had cleared the remains of the food away, nestling in close and favoring him with a brief kiss. "It's been too long since we've had this," he murmured.

"You've been busy," Kaidyn replied. "The infirmaries are fuller than they've been in years now that everyone is finally returning home. There aren't enough healers to go around."

"I know. Still, I would have liked to spend more time together earlier. I feel as though we've missed the best part of summer."

"Perhaps not the very best," Kaidyn told him, and turned to kiss him long and deep with the taste of honey still on their lips. His hands buried their way beneath Sorin's shirt.

"You certainly don't waste any time," came Sorin's response after Kaidyn eventually pulled away, though his cheeks were flushed and his breathing came heavier.

"No sense in waiting when I have you all to myself like this," Kaidyn grinned.

"Ah. You've brought us here to take advantage of me, then?"

"You are welcome to take advantage of me instead if you like," Kaidyn replied gallantly, and eased them both to the ground.

And because neither of them could be bothered with things like caution or decorum on such a fine day, because it had indeed been weeks since such an opportunity had presented itself, they did not wait for another.

They trusted that the rushing water and dappled shade

alone would be enough to cover their unashamedly bare flesh, unrestrained moans, and pleasantly sweaty tangle of limbs beneath a vast open sky.

"Sorin. Wake up, love." Kaidyn whispered the words close to his ear while running fingers through strands of dark hair.

Sorin groaned and stretched, his eyes fluttering open. "What time is it?" he mumbled.

"Near dusk. Time to go, I'm afraid." Kaidyn watched Sorin stretch again, yawning, and his gaze lingered on the grass stains marking what he could see of Sorin's pale flesh, recalling exactly how they had come to be there.

"You're staring at me. I can feel it," Sorin said as Kaidyn helped him up.

"So I am. And a lovely sight it is, too, if I may be so bold."

"I expect you may," Sorin returned, "since boldness has ever been your strong suit. And as it happens, Nora has said she can handle the infirmary without me at least for tonight. So if you have no other plans . . ."

"None besides your company," Kaidyn assured him, and Sorin slipped his hand into Kaidyn's as they left the river behind them.

Compared to the privacy of their afternoon, the town seemed even more bustling than usual, rapidly filling with the activity of early evening. It was still warm despite the hour as they made their way through the growing press of bodies, the sights and sounds of people meeting and chatting among themselves. They passed by busily opening and closing doors and shutters, the heat and smell of food cooking, and the high-pitched noises of children playing among themselves. Briefly, a memory bubbled to the surface—*he was running, boots pounding over dusty cobblestones, losing himself in the thick swarm of heat and bitterness that rose up to swallow him*—but Kaidyn blinked and the memory was gone, replaced by the easy warmth of Sorin's arm in his.

It was as they were passing by a tight-knit group of young women that Kaidyn heard the sound of his name spoken in furtive whispers, quickly followed by Sorin's. He glanced over, sure that Sorin must have heard it too and more, but he appeared unperturbed, making no attempt to either hide himself or hasten their steps. He was uncloaked, seemingly unbothered by the attention that his family name still afforded him.

"Do you know what they say about you?" Sorin asked him, once they could no longer feel the cluster of stares at their backs.

"What do they say?" Kaidyn asked, curiously.

"They say that you and your men single-handedly ended the war. That you fought like a man possessed and that your loyalty to your kingdom was such that you refused to die, even when instructed to do so by your betters."

Kaidyn snorted. "That's ridiculous. We didn't *win* anything — not even a fort. One tiny, ragtag army fought another equally small army to a standstill. And that had nothing to do with the end of the war. The timing was complete coincidence."

They were leaving the marketplace behind them now and Sorin's voice was quiet but clear in Kaidyn's ears, a smile hovering about his mouth. "That may be, but you of all people should know how stories are. They've a way of shaping themselves. Speaking of which, you've also been gifted a new name."

"Oh?"

"Kaidyn the Brave." The smile grew wider. "It suits you."

Kaidyn paused, unsure how he felt about this or whether or not he was being teased. " . . .It seems a little unoriginal," he said finally, and Sorin only laughed in response.

They continued on in companionable silence, the shadows

growing longer around them until Sorin eventually spoke again. "I received a letter yesterday," he said, and though his tone was still light, Kaidyn could hear the weight of the words behind it.

"Oh? From whom?"

"My mother and father. I had Nora read it to me. Father asks if I will soon return home. They worry about me, though I insisted they not visit me here. It is a long way to travel, and I . . .I wanted to have the chance to get used to things, before I met with them again," Sorin confessed.

"I see." Kaidyn was not sure if Sorin was telling him this simply because he had not had the time to talk to him about it sooner, or if it was something he had left purposefully un-said until now.

Sorin glanced fleetingly in Kaidyn's direction. "Both of them also ask about you."

"Me? What do they wish to know?"

"Like everyone else, they've heard of your courage and your skill with the sword. I have never told them in so many words, but I'm certain they know of us." It was hard to tell in the growing dimness, but Kaidyn was sure he spotted a faint blush dusting Sorin's cheeks. "They wanted me to ask you if, whenever I chose to return home, you wish to ac-company me," Sorin finished.

"Ah." Kaidyn's heart was suddenly beating twice as hard. "And what will you write in reply?"

"I don't yet know."

Sorin said nothing more. A hush fell over the two of them again, both men dwelling on their thoughts for several long minutes until Kaidyn took his turn to break the silence. "I have something to tell you also."

"What is it?"

Kaidyn passed a slightly nervous hand through his hair. "I've been granted a role in the Honor Guard, should I wish to accept such a post," he began, and watched Sorin nod.

"Nora told me. You should be proud of such an offer." He hesitated. "Would I be mistaken in believing your role would likely not involve combat?"

"You would not. Traditionally, the position of an Honor Guard is largely ceremonial. My first assignment would probably be to act as escort for the party traveling from Iskandir. The new king is said to be sending his own younger brother, Prince Daymon, as envoy—a gesture of good faith." Sorin waited, his expression betraying nothing as Kaidyn cleared his throat and went on. "It seems I am also to be knighted and given a title and land of my own, though I don't know whether I wish to accept either."

"Oh?"

"It all just seems so . . .unimportant somehow. I even thought about simply leaving such a life behind me and— well. I wouldn't know where to begin to look, or even if he's still alive, but it occurred to me I would have the freedom to search for my father now. If I truly wished to, that is. I could leave the capital—make my home elsewhere, or nowhere at all. Travel the kingdom, other kingdoms . . ."

Surprise, followed by something more, flashed briefly over Sorin's face. "I see we have some choices to make," he observed, and Kaidyn murmured his agreement, steering them smoothly out of the way of a pair of children who ran in front of their path.

Kaidyn wished he could tell exactly was going through Sorin's mind, yet he almost feared to ask. Their future together was something that had remained undiscussed until now—not because Kaidyn was afraid of whatever it might bring them but because, despite their newfound happiness, he could not help but feel a lingering sense of guilt.

It was not only that there was so much blood on his hands. He had led so many men to their deaths. He also felt remorse for the fact that, had it not been for him, Sorin would still have his sight. No matter how patient or determined, there were now many things that his lover would never be capable of doing again.

Sorin would never lie to him, and he had told Kaidyn he held no regrets, but even so . . .

His eyes fell to the wooden ring once again adorning Sorin's hand. The nobleman never removed it now, even when he slept.

Kaidyn had promised against all real hope to bring it back to Sorin, and so he had. But neither of them had brought up the second promise Kaidyn had made, which filled him with uncertainty. He wasn't sure if marriage was still something Sorin desired after such a momentous sacrifice on Kaidyn's behalf. The thought of the price his love had to pay made him question the worth of the sacrifice and whether he was worthy of Sorin at all. Kaidyn's bloodline and his honorary acceptance among the nobility had little to do with it, and everything to do with how he still saw himself. He was an unGifted soldier, plain and simple, with nothing else to offer. Sorin was far more than Kaidyn deserved, and always would be.

Nonetheless, it was a conversation Kaidyn knew they would need to have, and he was keenly aware there might never be a better opportunity than this.

They were alone on the path now, and Kaidyn steeled himself. "Sorin—"

"Kai, I—"

They both began talking in the same moment, and Sorin paused. "You first," he said quickly.

"No, please go ahead."

Sorin kept his eyes trained straight ahead of him, not turning toward Kaidyn as he spoke. "I have been thinking recently that I—well, there's something I have wanted to speak with you about, but there hasn't been . . .I have no desire to force the issue if —"

It had been a long time indeed since Kaidyn had seen Sorin so unsure of himself. "If you would rather not speak of this now . . ." Kaidyn began to suggest, but Sorin shook his head.

"I must. Kai, you need to know that you should not feel obligated in any way. You have a whole new life to become used to now that old prejudices are beginning to be torn away." He stopped, still not looking in Kaidyn's direction. "There is no reason for you to be tied to —"

"Sorin, no!" Kaidyn interrupted him. "Not once have I even considered — I have never thought of you as an obligation. I never will."

"But you do still feel shame," Sorin said, the words matter-of-fact.

"I . . .it's not . . ." But there was no way to deny this. Kaidyn stepped in front of Sorin to face him directly, feeling he had to explain himself in full. He owed Sorin that, no matter what. "I should have died that day. I would be gone now along with many of my men had it not been for what you did. I am the cause of your blindness," he said bluntly, searching Sorin's expression. "My very life is a gift from you. But I sometimes think I am not worthy of such a gift, much less . . ."

Sorin frowned. "Much less what?"

Kaidyn took a breath, steadying himself. "The day I left, I swore to you two things. Do you remember them?"

"I remember."

"Then you will know why I have not yet kept the second of my promises. It is not I who would be tied down, but the other way around."

"I see." Sorin's voice had gone low. "And do you truly think so little of yourself, even now? You, who have given so much for your country in spite of how it has treated you in return?" He had turned to stare in Kaidyn's direction, his face grown hard. "You believe your life to be so insignificant, that your own sacrifice is somehow less deserving than mine?" he continued, and he let go of Kaidyn, taking a step back.

Kaidyn struggled to explain himself. "You don't understand, I have not—"

"No. I understand you perfectly." Sorin was unmistakably angry now. "It is you who does not understand the worth of your own existence. The worth *I* place on it—assuming such things could even be measured."

"That isn't what I—"

"Do you love me?" Sorin asked abruptly.

"I—what?" The question halted Kaidyn's half-formed protestations in their tracks.

"Answer me true. Do you love me?" Sorin demanded again.

He did not have to think. "You know that I do."

"Then leave, right now, if you think I love you any less than I once did. I mean it. Leave, and I will find my own way home."

Kaidyn did not move. The silence stretched out.

"Kai?" Sorin's voice held no hesitation.

"I'm still here."

"Good." Sorin closed the distance between them again, feeling out for the shape of Kaidyn's fingers and twining them about his own. "Marry me, then."

Kaidyn could not seem to stop staring at him. "Sorin, I . . . are you sure of—"

"Ask me that ever again and you will be sorrier than you know. Yes, I am sure. Surer than anything I have been in my life." Despite his words, the brief moment of anger had fled from Sorin's voice, and there was now nothing there but quiet certainty as he rested his head on Kaidyn's shoulder. "I love you, Kai. Here or anywhere else, I want to spend the rest of my life by your side. If you will have me there." He lifted his head to gaze up at Kaidyn, turning it into a question—as though Kaidyn was capable of doing anything, saying anything else but for the single word he had once given in response to a similar request.

Be with me. It was like a lifetime ago. And just like then, Kaidyn had only one answer for him.

"Yes," he breathed into the stillness. "*Yes.*"

There were questions Kaidyn knew he should by rights be asking himself—questions he would once have shied from. Where would they go? What would they do? Would the world, changing though it was, accept them so readily?

It did not matter. None of it did—not while he held Sorin in his arms and felt the steady rhythm of his heart against his own, the truth of the words reverberating through him.

The shadows were growing longer as night fell gradually over the town, but he did not care. The darkness would not trouble him, nor would the dawn that followed.

They had all the time in the world.

You may also enjoy the following from eXtasy Books Inc:

A Trust to Follow
Diana Waters

Excerpt

"You! Wake up!" Something was being held under his nose.

Daymon gagged, his body jerking back to life. His eyes slid open, feeling gritty and heavy, and he could see he was in some kind of cell. The light was dim, and it took him several moments for the figures in front of him to steady.

"Good, you're awake. Drink up."

"Wha—"

There was no time to say anything else. A man, different from the one who had captured him, held Daymon roughly as he tried to struggle, yanking his hair back so that his face was jerked toward the ceiling. The man spoke again, this time to his companion. "Make him drink. No need to be gentle about it."

A second figure, lean and scrawny-looking, took the cup and held Daymon's nose. Daymon pressed his lips together, but his head was pounding, and his vision was already growing fuzzy at the lack of air. The need for oxygen made him gasp against his will, and in an instant, the foul-smelling liquid was being forced down his throat. Daymon managed to spit some of it back out, but the hard grip on his hair prevented him from going anywhere. His eyes watered as he choked but swallowed the rest, hating himself for it.

"That's enough," the first of them said finally. "Too much of that and he won't be waking up at all." Without further comment, both of them turned to walk away.

"Wait! What did you make me drink?"

The first man kept walking, but the second stopped to smile at Daymon in a way that made his skin crawl.

"Just a little something to keep you good and quiet. Can't have you turning into a monster and destroying the place, can we? No, you'll stay put until we're ready to hand you over to someone who'll be able to take proper care of you."

"Shut up and keep walking," the other growled, and his partner shrugged and obeyed. The gate crashed closed behind them, followed by the sounds of a heavy lock being closed with a sharp grating.

Daymon tried to stand as he heard their footsteps echo away, but instead found himself on hands and knees without knowing exactly how he had gotten there. In fact, he couldn't even seem to see straight ahead anymore, let alone stand. The room wavered before his eyes, looking for all the world as though it was leaning to and fro. Could he be on a boat? But no, that couldn't be right. Daymon had been on plenty of boats before, and this was not the same sensation he felt while on the water. Besides, the floor beneath his hands was not wood, nor was it stone. The floor seemed to be made of densely packed, unyielding earth.

Magic. He needed to use it now before his body could give out completely. He might be lacking in physical strength, but this was the one thing he still had some shred of control over. He could still sense it, somewhere deep beneath his skin. If he could just manage to reach it, draw it out—

But like water through his fingers, it slid from his grasp

the more he attempted to hold onto it, and Daymon's eyes were trying to close on their own. He had failed, not only himself but Rhyder as well.

He registered the muffled thump his body made as he fell on his side, but felt nothing more than the vague coolness of the earth beneath him. At least there was no pain, he thought distantly. Lapsing into unconsciousness, he began planning his escape route. He would summon all of his magic to bring the place crashing down, he decided, and nobody would be able to stop him then. When I wake up . . . yes, as soon as I wake up again . . .

It grew dark for a time, and when Daymon opened his eyes again, he was alone. All was quiet. His head continued to throb unmercifully, but the cold, the dreadful cold, was worse. He glanced down and saw that he had been stripped of his clothing. His breath hitched in his throat. Surely not— they would never—no.

"Calm down, just calm down," Daymon told himself under his breath. He was eventually able to make himself stop shivering by drawing his knees up to his chest and winding his arms tightly around his legs. No. He would have known if they had . . . there was pain, yes, but not that kind of pain. They were just trying to frighten him. Intimidate him. Scare tactics, which Daymon was smart enough to recognize and ignore.

Less easy to ignore was the gaping silence that exposed his own weakness. Guilt at his shortcomings which had led him here in the first place and nameless fears threatening to overwhelm him set Daymon's heart pounding. He attempted to distract himself by wondering what would happen to him next.

In the eyes of these people, he was worth something— obviously. So Daymon was sure he would not be killed anytime in the near future. He would probably not even be seriously harmed. Had they wished, his captors could have easily already done so, which likely meant that he was being kept whole for something, or someone, else. He was well aware that any number of people, or even whole kingdoms, would pay handsomely for a young Evoker of royal blood.

The thought was not exactly reassuring. More comforting were thoughts of Rhyder. Even now, the heroic soldier was likely putting those famous skills of his to work, tracking Daymon down and coming up with a plan to get him back. The use of Daymon's magic seemed ill-advised in light of that. There was as great a chance of bringing this whole place down on top of him as there was of freeing himself.

In any case, Daymon was no longer sure his magic was an option. Something felt off, like a part of him was missing. The low murmuring, like the rush of water from somewhere on the edge of his hearing, wasn't there like it should have been. Instead, there was only silence, the creeping nausea of a too-empty stomach, and the dull throbbing of his head keeping time with his heartbeat.

His spine was growing stiff from curling forward. Despite the cold, Daymon made himself get up and walk a few steps to stretch his legs and back a little. His shivering had returned in full force now that there was less body heat to draw from, but it couldn't be helped. Now that he was standing, he realized that he badly needed to relieve himself. He looked around again just in case he had overlooked something, but his cell was utterly bare. There was nothing to cover himself with, let alone a container to use as a chamber pot. Daymon sat once more, in the same position as he had previously in an attempt to warm himself and waited. And waited. Abandoned in the dark, he was as helpless as a child.

Nothing. Not a single footstep from anywhere around Daymon. Not so much as a whisper to confirm that anyone was around for miles. Perhaps there isn't, he thought with a jolt. Maybe they meant to leave him here until someone came to claim him. He could truly be alone, for the first time in his entire life.

But no, that was foolish of him to imagine. There must at least be guards somewhere out there. They wouldn't risk leaving him like that. Likely the absence of sound was some other scare tactic of theirs, and he wouldn't allow it to frighten him. He was good at waiting. However, the fact remained that his stomach was beginning to cramp.

It was humiliating, relieving himself in the far corner like an animal, and such was undoubtedly the point. They might not be able to afford to hurt Daymon too much, but that didn't mean they couldn't have their fun with him in other small, petty ways. His life would be spared, but his dignity would not be. Daymon resolved not to let it faze him, and he resolutely turned his face away from the mess. His cell was small enough that he could already smell it, but he would put up with it. What other choice did he have?

ABOUT THE AUTHOR

Diana is a New Zealander currently living in rural Japan. She has no idea where in the world she'll be this time next year and is pretty okay with that. Other than reading and writing, her main passions include travel, amateur photography, and competitive swimming.